The Middle-Aged Amish Widow

Expectant Amish Widows Book 10

Samantha Price

Chapter 1

This is the day which the LORD hath made;
we will rejoice and be glad in it.
Psalm 118:24

"At least you'll be able to rest now."

Sarah Hersler sniffed and looked across at her closest friend, Naomi. "I don't need to rest. I wanted him to get better, or just stay with me if he didn't."

Naomi grabbed Sarah's hand. "He didn't get better, not in this world. Now he's pain-free and he's at peace. Think of it that way. I know it's hard—not that I've ever lost a husband, but I've had plenty of people close to me die."

Sarah nodded knowing that Naomi's mother had died only six months ago. "I will, but it'll take time to adjust to him being gone. We married at eighteen and now I'm past forty. I've been married to him longer than I haven't been—over twenty years." Sarah looked around her living room, her eyes wandering toward the window, to the couch by the window where Thomas had taken to sleeping when he could no longer walk up the stairs.

Thomas had needed a lot of looking after, and at times it'd been tiring, but she would've carried on forever. God had taken him home a week ago, and earlier that day he'd been buried. And now the, almost- two- hundred, visitors for the after-funeral gathering had left the house.

"What are you thinking?"

"Just that I won't know what to do with myself."

"You can do anything you want now. The first thing you should do is take a rest. Maybe go somewhere for a vacation."

"I couldn't. Maybe later, but not at the moment."

"You've worn yourself away to a shadow. There's barely anything of you.

You could stay with Grace. She's always asking you to stay."

Grace was the sister that Sarah felt closest to, but she also lived the furthest away—too far to come back for Thomas' funeral. "It'd be too much effort to get there and that would outweigh any benefit of the rest."

"That's true. Abe and I will look after your place if you want to go somewhere."

"Denke. I know you will." As much as she liked Naomi, all she wanted right now was to be left alone. Yes, she wanted to feel sorry for herself and think about how things used to be with Thomas back before he fell ill and needed constant care. "Do you want a cup of tea or anything?"

"Nee. I'm fine. I'll clean up and then I'll go unless you want me to stay longer. I've got Abe looking after the children."

"Nee, don't worry. The ladies did most of it before they left. There are only those few plates to wash."

"You know where I am if you need me. Come over if you want some company. I'll send the children outside so it'll be a little quieter. And " Naomi laughed.

"I'll be okay. I'll come over and see you tomorrow."

"You will?"

"Yes I will. It's lonely here without him." She couldn't help her eyes going back to the couch by the window."

At that moment she was pleased she didn't have any children because they would've lost their father. She buried her face in her hands for having such a silly thought. She and Thomas had tried to have children for years but could never have any. And then Thomas fell ill. And it went completely out of her mind. This was the first time she thought about it in years. Now she was seeing it as being a blessing rather than a curse.

She had grown up with Naomi and had watched her bear six children while Thomas and she had gone without. It had been difficult to have feelings of joy for her friend while burying her own wretched unhappiness. Why does God bless some and not others?

Naomi came out of the kitchen and Sarah stared at her. Sarah realized she'd been in a daze and hadn't even known that her friend had gotten up off the couch next to her.

"Are you alright?"

"I guess so. I have to be don't I?"

"Jah, you have to look after yourself for the sake of your child."

Sarah's hand went to her stomach. News of her pregnancy had put a smile on her husband's lips. They'd found out a few weeks before he'd died. He knew he wasn't going to see his child grow up, so he wrote the child a letter. Sarah kept the letter safe in her bedroom.

Naomi was the only other person with whom Sarah had shared the good news.

"I don't like leaving you. Do you want to come home with us?" Naomi asked.

"Nee, I'm okay but myself. I'm alright by myself. I just have to get used to it."

"Is that a car?"

"I think so; it sounds like one." Naomi jumped up off the couch and hurried over to the window. *"Ach, nee!"*

"Who is it?"

"Your *mudder!* "

"She said she wasn't coming and she's missed the whole thing."

"I'm going out the back way. I hope everything goes alright."

Naomi left. Sarah rested a hand on her belly, and wished she could join her.

She opened her front door and the taxi driver dropped her mother's bag at her feet. Then her mother walked over and looked her daughter up and down.

"The funeral was at ten o'clock this morning. You've missed the whole thing. Did you get the dates wrong?"

"I told you a long time ago that the next funeral I'd go to will be my own."

"Sarah looked out down at the bag. "How long are you staying?"

"I thought now that Thomas is gone you could look after me."

"Why is that? Are you sick?"

"Nee, just old."

"Are you moving here? How long are you staying?"

"I thought I would move in with you." Her mother suddenly focused on something on Sarah's shoulder, then leaned in and brushed something off the shoulder of her dress.

Sarah looked down. "There's nothing there."

"Not now, but there was."

Sarah frowned at her mother.

"There was some lint. Now, let's go inside."

"Should we talk about this, or something?" Sarah asked hopefully.

"We're talking about it now, aren't we? Be a good girl and take my bag to my room."

Chapter 2

But let all those that put their trust in thee rejoice:
let them ever shout for joy,
because thou defendest them:
*let them also that **love** thy name be joyful in thee.*
Psalm 5:11

The next day over breakfast, Sarah decided to tell her mother her good news. Aside from Sarah telling Naomi, she and Thomas had kept the news to themselves, but now it was about time that she let those closest to her share some good news.

Her mother's mouth fell open and she did not look happy. "You're having a what?"

"A *boppli*."

"Are you trying to tell a joke, Sarah? It's not funny."

"*Nee!* This is not a joke or anything, *Mamm*. Thomas and I thought we'd never be able to have one, but," Sarah started crying, "now he won't be here to raise his *kin.*"

9

"Stop blubbering, girl. Exactly what's the problem?

"There is no problem."

"Well I have one."

"What problem do you have, *Mamm?*"

"I'm not sharing the house with an infant. I have raised twelve *kinner* and I'm not going to go through any more sleepless nights. You're simply going to have to build on to the house."

"What?"

"A *grossdaddi haus.* Everyone's got one. I think it odd that you and Tom didn't bother to build one on for me."

Sarah hated it when her mother referred to Thomas as Tom. No one else ever called him Tom, only her mother. "He had other things on his mind, like trying to keep well."

"He can't have been *too* sick!" Her mother stared at Sarah's stomach. Her left eyebrow was arched nearly to her prayer *kapp* and the corners of her mouth turned down disapprovingly.

Sarah squirmed in her chair. "I can't afford to

build one on, so it's out of the question. You might be more comfortable in your own *haus*. Or maybe you could move in with Liz."

"That won't do. Liz and Liam have talked about having Liam's *vadder* move in with them."

Smart move, Sarah thought while watching her mother's mouth forming words.

"We can simply sell my *haus* and I'll be kind enough to give you the money to build on the *grossdaddi haus.*"

"Don't you want your *haus* to be there so you can go back there?"

"There's only one place I'm going at my age. I've made the long trip here and I don't intend on going back. I thought you'd be pleased to have me, now that Tom's gone. We can keep each other company."

Sarah stared at her mother as though in a trance.

Her mother repeated, "I'm not going back."

"So you've intended to sell your place all along. You've just up and left it without making arrangements to lease or sell it? Or have you done that?"

"Don't look at me like that. You can go there and arrange for it to be sold. I was going to lease it out, but since Tom left you with no money I suppose I'll have to make the sacrifice of selling my *haus*. I don't know what the rest of my *kinner* will think when I go to *Gott* and all my money will be tied up in your *haus*. It'll hardly be fair."

"That's true. Maybe you could call them and see if one of them would prefer to build onto their home. I truly don't mind."

"They've all got families, but you're alone. Or, I thought you'd be alone. How long have you got to go?"

"A few months—around six."

Her mother shook her head in disgust.

"It's a happy occasion, *Mamm*. Please don't act like it's not *gut* news. Having a *boppli* is what I've always wanted."

"I can't see why you could want something like that. Having one at your age is outrageous."

"I'm only in my forties. That's not old at all."

"It is to be having your first one. And having one with no husband will be a bit odd."

"There's nothing I can do about either one, except to trust *Gott* that this is His plan for me."

"What are you going to live on, then?"

"I told you already, Thomas and I have savings."

"You do? But not enough to build that extension on your *haus* for me?"

"Jah, that's right."

"The *haus* might take a while to sell. You should go there before you get bigger and people find out."

"It's nothing to be ashamed of."

"You're too old to be in the 'family way.'"

"It's perfectly acceptable these days to use the word 'pregnant.'"

"I don't like that word. It sounds vulgar."

"You want me to go there—to your *haus?"*

"Jah. I don't want *you* to sell the house; a realtor can do that, but I want you to find the realtor who can make all the arrangements."

Sarah breathed out heavily and nodded. "Okay."

"Okay, you'll do it? Or okay you'll think about

it?"

"I'll do it." A few days away from her mother, right now, felt like a pretty good thing."

* * *

"Pssst!"

Sarah looked up to see Naomi outside the kitchen window. She beckoned her in before she got up from the kitchen table to open the back door.

"It's safe; she's asleep," Sarah said.

"Gut! It's really safe to come in?"

"Jah. She's a sound sleeper."

"What's she doing here?" Naomi whispered as she walked with Sarah into the kitchen.

Sarah slumped into a chair. "She wants to stay."

"Nee!" Naomi sat opposite her. "Why?"

Sarah shrugged. "Who knows? I told her about the *boppli* and now she wants me to build a *grossdaddi haus* on for her. She said she doesn't want to hear the child crying all the time."

"Why you? Why not your *bruder* or one of your

schweschders?"

"I think they've all made excuses and I lost out because I couldn't think of one quick enough. I wish they'd warned me."

Naomi shook her head.

"She wants me to go back to Ohio, to sell her *haus,* so there'll be money enough to build."

"That means she'll be here forever and just when you're supposed to be taking a breather."

"I know. I wanted to get used to Thomas being gone, in peace." Sarah nibbled a fingernail wondering if there was any other way around things. With her hand against her chest, Sarah said, "It's too much. I feel I've got nothing left to give."

"Especially not to her."

Sarah's jaw dropped open.

"I'm sorry, that was mean. I shouldn't have said it. I know she's your *mudder,* but she makes everyone around her miserable."

"She's got high expectations."

"Can't you think of a way out?"

Sarah shook her head. *"Nee,* I can't."

15

Chapter 3

And not only so, but we glory in tribulations also:
knowing that tribulation worketh patience;
Romans 5:3

Sarah's mother, Ruth, had moved away from Lancaster County years ago—around the same time that Sarah had gotten married.

Sarah had only visited her mother once in the past five years. Sarah's mother and Thomas had never gotten along very well. It had been easier to keep the two of them apart, and the best way of doing that had been to keep distance between them. Thomas had objected to his mother-in-law being so forthright and opinionated about her grown daughter's life.

It was a long bus ride from Lancaster County to Ohio. When the taxi that took Sarah from the bus stop pulled up in the driveway of her mother's house, she was faced with an unexpected sight. The house sorely needed a coat of paint and the garden looked dreadful. She hoped that was all her mother had been talking about when she spoke of the "few things" that needed repair. If there was any work that needed to be done inside, as well as what she could see on the outside, it might mean that she'd have to stay there for longer than she'd planned.

After the taxi drove away, she placed her suitcase down by the door and searched for the hidden front-door key. She found it under a rock near the first step, just where her mother had told her it would be.

Sarah heaved a relieved sigh. She wouldn't have wanted to come all this way and be locked out of the house. Pushing the door open, she stepped inside and looked around to see why her mother had been so vague about what needed doing. The first thing she noticed was a large water stain on the ceiling of the living room. Holding her head, she hoped the roof wouldn't need replacing—that would be costly. Sarah calmed down when she realized it might only need a small repair. Now standing under the stain she saw that it had dried out. *Hopefully, an old leak that Mamm has since gotten fixed.*

She took a deep breath and ventured into the kitchen. There she saw tiles missing at the back of the sink and the stove, and some handles of cupboards missing. When she opened one cupboard door, it fell down hanging on one hinge only. *Okay, a little work in the kitchen too.* After she did a quick look into all four bedrooms upstairs and the one bathroom downstairs, she knew without a doubt that she'd be overseeing this work for weeks.

Sarah walked into the living room and sank into a chair. Naomi had told her right after the funeral that this was *her* time. She hadn't even gotten one day to herself. After Thomas had died, it was the funeral arrangements and organizing her house for the many visitors she knew she was going to have the day before and the day of the funeral. Then there was her mother's surprise arrival, landing on her doorstep. It was too much. Sarah knew why her mother had chosen to live with her rather than one of her other siblings. It was because she had no children. Her mother wasn't the typical grandmotherly kind.

Sarah shook herself out of her dark mood and reminded herself that she had one good and precious thing in her life. God had finally answered Thomas' and her prayers, and she would soon be a mother—she couldn't let anything weigh her down. She had to stay strong for her baby.

Naomi had told her to take a vacation; so Sarah would make this stay at her mother's a vacation. Maybe she should stay a little longer than she'd planned. That way she'd have a little more time away from her mother and her demanding ways.

Now, taking another look around the living room, she just hoped her mother had enough money in the bank for all the repairs. She'd go to the barn and call Naomi and have her pass on a message to her mother. Perhaps her mother had left bank details in the house somewhere, or had money hidden away. Naomi wouldn't like having to go and talk to her mother, but Sarah couldn't think of any other way around it.

* * *

She picked up the phone in her mother's barn and dialed Naomi's number, which she knew by heart.

"Naomi, it's me."

"You got there okay?" Naomi asked.

"I did, but I need to you to ask my *mudder* something for me."

"You want me to go there?"

Sarah said, *"Jah,* I need you to ask her something."

"I'll do it for you, but you know how she speaks to me." Naomi's voice had gone from normal to whining.

"Jah, don't worry, she's like that with everyone; it's not just you. She doesn't know she's doing it."

"That doesn't make it right."

"I'm sorry. Can you help me?"

"Okay, I'll do it for you." Naomi heaved a sigh. "What do I need to ask her?"

"Denke. Ask her if I can take money out of her bank account to do the *haus* repairs. When she says yes, ask her where her bank book is." Saying that

out aloud, Sarah felt a little foolish and unorganized that they were only now thinking about the cost of the repairs. All of this should have been sorted out before she left home.

"I'll ask her, and then do you want me to call you back?"

"Jah." Sarah gave Naomi her mother's phone number and waited by the phone in the barn for Naomi to call her back. She figured it would take fifteen minutes for Naomi to walk next door, talk to her mother and then walk back.

The phone rang again; it had taken a little longer than Sarah had anticipated. "Naomi?"

"Jah, it's me."

"What did she say?" Sarah asked.

"She said she hasn't got any money. That's why she needs to sell the *haus."*

What? Sarah rubbed her forehead. How did her mother expect her to find the money—out of thin air?

"Sarah, are you there?"

"Jah, I'm just having a little panic attack that's

22

all."

"She said to use a builder friend of hers. His name is Isaac King and she said to give you his address. Do you have a pen?"

"I do, but does she want me to pay for the repairs?"

"I can loan you some money if you need it, Sarah."

"*Nee,* that's okay, *denke.* I guess I'll have to use my savings and *Mamm* can pay me back when the *haus* is sold." That was the only solution and that explained why her mother had been 'fuzzy' about things.

Naomi gave Sarah Isaac King's address.

"*Denke* for keeping an eye on *Mamm* while I'm gone, Naomi."

"I'm happy to do that—from a distance. Don't worry about things here. You just try to relax and have a good time."

"I'll try." Sarah heaved a sigh and then said goodbye to her friend before she replaced the receiver.

Then, Sarah walked into the paddock and slipped a rope around her mother's horse.

She reminded herself to tell the boy next door that he didn't need to feed the horse while she was there. After she hitched the buggy, she headed to the address that Naomi had given her for the builder. She wondered whether Isaac King was a part of the community and if that was how her mother knew him. The name wasn't familiar to her, but she had only made a handful of visits to her mother in all the years that her mother had lived there. She just hoped that the man was reliable, and available to commence work soon.

When she found the address, she passed a buggy that had just come from the house. There was a woman in the buggy and she looked upset.

Chapter 4

*Be glad then, you children of Zion, And rejoice in the
Lord your God; For He has given you the former rain
faithfully, And He will cause the rain to come down
for you— The former rain, And the latter rain in the
first month.*
Joel 2: 23

Isaac King was happy to close the door on Nancy
Hostetler. He placed the pie she'd made him
alongside the three pies he'd gotten in the past two
days—all from single ladies.

Being a widower for two years now, he got
plenty of attention from the mature single ladies
in the community who thought he needed fattening
up, or perhaps they were trying to soften his heart
with their cooking skills.

Nancy had asked to come inside, but Isaac had
said he was just leaving to do some work on a
new job he'd just secured. He stood in his kitchen,
hands on hips, looking at his baked goods sitting

on the counter like ducks in a row.

The sound of a buggy made his heart beat faster in fear. Was that Nancy coming back again, and if so, what did she want this time? There were only so many ways a man could convey to a lady that he wasn't interested.

He was pleased when he looked out the window and saw that it wasn't Nancy. Squinting at the driver of the buggy he saw another woman. His shoulders drooped. Would he have to move—find somewhere else to live? Should he just not answer the door? He couldn't do that; he had to go through with it and answer the door. Why couldn't they leave him alone? He didn't think himself a handsome man and there wasn't anything particularly special about him. What was it that attracted all these women to his door?

She knocked on the door. Rat-a-tat-tat. Even the sound of the knock annoyed him. He glanced up at the ceiling. *Give me patience, Lord.* He placed his hand on the handle of the door and slowly opened it, reminding himself to wedge himself in the doorway in case the lady tried to walk inside. As he did so, he was surprised to see he didn't readily know this lady, yet she was vaguely familiar.

"Hello," she said sweetly.

She was an attractive woman, and if he ever intended on being even the slightest bit interested in another woman, he would've been pleased that she'd knocked on his door. He shook his head. "Please, no more pies. I have plenty—too many in fact."

The woman laughed, showing her even white teeth while her bright blue eyes crinkled at the corners. "I don't have any pies. My *mudder* sent me here."

He took a better look at the horse and buggy. It was Ruth Eicher's horse and buggy.

"I'm looking for Isaac King," she said.

He opened his mouth to speak but no words came out. He couldn't believe he'd been so carelessly rude to Ruth's daughter. Being rude at all was the opposite of how he wanted to be perceived.

The attractive woman continued to speak. "My

mudder sent me here. She said you could do some building work for me, well, for her actually. Her name is Ruth Eicher. I hope you know her or I might have the wrong address."

"You're Ruth Eicher's *dochder?* I thought I recognized you. She wants me to do some work on her *haus?* " His face lit up.

"Jah, I am her *dochder,* Sarah Hersler, and *jah,* she does."

"Gut. Come inside." He stood back and flung the door open. "How is your *mudder*?"

Sarah stepped through the door. "She's moved in with me. I live in Lancaster County."

"She's gone? Since when?"

"She arrived a few days ago."

"She didn't say goodbye."

"Knowing my *mudder,* it was probably a sudden decision."

"You said she wants me to do something?"

"She asked me to come here to see if you'd do some work on her *haus* because she wants to sell it and then move into my *haus.* Also, she's done things backwards and moved first before she sold her place."

He laughed heartily. "That sounds like Ruth all right."

"She said she wanted you to do the work if you can. Will I have to wait for you to do it?" Sarah put her fingertips to her lips. "I'm sorry. I'm messing this all up. I'm not sure what the right thing is to say. My husband has always done these things for me."

Here was one woman he wouldn't have to be wary around because she was married. "And you're here by yourself?"

"I am."

"Are you in a hurry?" he asked.

"Nee, I've got all the time in the world."

"Fancy a slice of pecan pie, Mrs. Hersler?"

"I'd love some."

Sarah stared at the row of pies on his kitchen counter, suddenly feeling hungry.

When Sarah sat down at the kitchen table, Isaac cut a slice of pie. "Why don't I remember you ever visiting your *mudder?*"

"I'm not certain. I don't recall you being here either."

"When were you here last?"

She shook her head. "I don't know. Maybe it was longer than I thought. Maybe two years, maybe five. Time has a way of getting away from me."

"I only became friendlier with your *mudder* after my *fraa,* Veronica, died. Your *mudder* was such a blessing and a comfort to me."

"I'm sorry to hear about your *fraa.*"

He looked down and nodded.

She added, "My *mudder?* You found her comforting?"

"Jah, she's a caring woman much like my own *mudder* was. I'll miss her, as will everyone else in this community. She'll be a blessing to you."

Were they talking about the same woman? "My mother is Ruth Eicher, and she was married to Hezekiah Eicher."

He chuckled. *"Jah,* I know. We're talking about the same person. And that's her horse and buggy out there. I recognized the horse as soon as I saw him."

Sarah nodded, wondering how there could be such varied opinions about her mother. She could barely make her friend deliver a message to her, and now this man was all but singing her praises.

When he sat down with her, he said, "I can come by this afternoon, see what needs to be done, and then I'll work out some costs."

"So you can start on it soon?" *The sooner the better.*

"*Jah,* I don't have anything urgent to do at this time."

"*Gut!* That works out well." Sarah noticed that he wasn't eating. "You're not joining me? I don't want to be the only one eating." Sarah gave an embarrassed giggle at the way she'd been hungrily attacking the pie.

"*Nee,* sometimes you get to the point where you just have too much pie." He glanced at the other pies.

"*Jah,* I've noticed you've got quite a few."

Sarah spent the next few minutes telling Isaac everything she'd seen that needed repairing in her mother's house.

"Why don't I stop by first thing in the morning? It's getting late in the day and I'd rather do my investigations in the strong light of the day."

"Okay." Sarah nodded, thinking she'd have to go into town and draw some money out of the bank so he'd have the needed cash to start buying materials. "What time approximately might you be there? Early morning or late?"

"I've got a few lose ends to tie up on a job I've just finished. Why don't we make it eleven?"

"Perfect." Sarah looked down at her empty plate and suddenly felt awkward. She didn't know this man and had no idea what else to talk about with him. "Well, *denke* for the pie."

He laughed as his eyes flickered to her empty plate. "You seemed to enjoy it. Would you like to take the rest?"

Sarah couldn't work out why he had so many pies if he didn't eat them. *"Nee, denke."*

He rose to his feet and took hold of one of the pies. "Why don't you take this one at least? I won't eat it and it'll only go to waste."

"Are you certain? I don't like to see anything wasted."

He chuckled. "I'm certain."

She stood up and pushed her chair under the table, and went to pick up her empty plate to carry it to the sink.

"Nee, leave it."

She looked up at him. He was at least five inches taller than herself and she wasn't a short woman. He was still smiling at her.

"Okay. I'll see you tomorrow morning then."

"I'll walk you out." He carried the pie to the buggy for her and placed it on the seat next to her.

"I'm so pleased you can do the repairs at such short notice."

He laughed. "I don't do so much these days. Just the odd job here and there."

She clicked the horse forward, turned the buggy around, and headed toward the road.

Chapter 5

And he saith unto them,
Ye shall drink indeed of my cup,
and be baptized with the baptism that I
am baptized with: but to sit on my right
hand, and on my left, is not mine to give,
but it shall be given to them for
whom it is prepared of my Father.
Matthew 20:23

"*Denke* for coming here, Isaac." Sarah said, as she stood next to him. They stood side-by-side on the porch, staring into Ruth's house.

"Eleven o'clock in the morning isn't exactly early for me," he said with a smile.

"What I meant to say is *denke* for putting this as a priority and leaving your other jobs so that you could do this one."

"I told you yesterday, I'm not working much and besides that I've just finished up a job. Anyway, even if I was busy, I'd be happy to do this job.

Anything for Ruth."

She eyed him suspiciously, wondering if he were being sarcastic. "You certainly speak highly of my *mudder*. It's nice of you."

"See how nice you think I am when you get the quote." He laughed. "From what you said there's a lot of work to be done inside."

"Don't worry about a quote. My *mudder* was adamant that you were the only person she wanted to do the work. She wouldn't hear of getting a quote from another builder."

"Rest assured I'll do it for as little as I possibly can. I won't charge Ruth for the labor, just for the materials."

"Nee, that's too generous. This is your livelihood; my *mudder* wouldn't expect you to charge so little."

"It would be a crime if I charged Ruth. She's been a good friend to me and this is a small way I can do something for her. As I told you yesterday, I don't do a lot of jobs these days. It's not as though I have a *familye* to spend time with."

Sarah looked at the man's face. She couldn't

speak for her mother; if the man wanted to do things that way, who was she to tell him otherwise? "Come inside and see the rest of the *haus*. You might change your mind."

"After you."

Sarah led the way inside.

Holding a notebook and pen in one hand, Isaac took his hat off with the other hand and placed it on the table inside the door. "She never had people inside the house, she told me, and now I can see why," Isaac said as he stood in the center of the house looking around.

"I left it too long to visit her. I should've come more often. It was hard though, with my husband being ill for so long."

"I'm sorry to hear that. I hope he's better now."

"He's… " Sarah didn't finish her words because Isaac King wasn't really listening; he was already walking into the kitchen, alternately looking up at the ceiling and the cabinets, and jotting on his notepad.

He swung around and stared at her. "If Ruth had

said the word, the community would've come and fixed the place for her. No one should live in a state like this."

She looked at the floor, embarrassed that her mother had been living in a house in such ill repair.

Sarah continued to follow Isaac around the house as he made notes. When he was done, he stood at the foot of the stairs.

"How long did you say you're staying here?"

"I'll stay here until the work is finished."

He scratched his head. "I hope you're prepared for a long stay."

"I am. My *mudder* is at home looking after things. I'm able to stay until the work is done and to do anything that you need me to do to help."

"That's good." He nodded. "Now I'll go away and work out some estimates for materials. And I'll work out how long everything might take so you'll be able to let your husband know how long you'll be here for."

"*Nee,* I don't..." She didn't finish her sentence because, once again, the man wasn't listening; he was concentrating on his notes. "Would you care for a cup of tea, Isaac?"

"Could I be rude and ask for a cup of *kaffe?*"

Sarah laughed. "That's not rude at all. I'll fix you one."

Sarah sipped her tea and looked across at the handsome stranger with the green twinkling eyes. "Can I ask you something, Isaac?"

"Of course, ask away."

"Why do you have so many pies at your *haus* when you don't like them?"

He burst out laughing and then stopped abruptly. "That's a very *gut* question. My wife, Veronica, died two years ago. I guess now some women think enough time has passed for me to get married again and that's where all the pies are coming from."

"From women who want to capture your heart?"

"That's one way to put it."

"I'm sorry to hear about your *fraa*. It's never easy when someone close to you dies."

"*Jah*. Your *vadder* died not long ago."

"A few years, and it's still not easy. People who

leave us go to a better place, but that doesn't make it easier for those who are left behind with holes in their hearts."

"Exactly, Sarah. And a place that can never be filled by another. Your *mudder* knows that pain, perhaps that's why we connect on some level."

"Can I ask how your wife died? She must've been fairly young."

Isaac looked into the dark reflections of his coffee, thinking about Veronica and how he missed her laugh and her liveliness. She'd lit up his life like a beacon and without her; he seemed to be living life in the shadows. The stream of women vying for his affections had only increased the pain in his heart.

"She died in childbirth and the child went with her. It was to be our first *kinner.*" He licked his dry lips. Everyone around him knew his story and Sarah was the first person he'd had to tell it to.

"I'm so sorry to hear that. That must be something you live with every day."

He blinked in an effort to keep back tears.

"I do. We were ten years hoping for a child. Veronica was such a happy woman, she didn't let me see her pain and sorrow at seeing her friends and sisters have babies. I could feel her pain, but she kept it from me." He looked up at Sarah and saw huge blue eyes and he knew that Sarah had a true heart and was full of kindness—like Ruth, her mother.

"Sounds like she was a special woman."

"You see she had such pain in her heart and she knew I would share her pain, and she didn't want that. I think she didn't want to upset me." He laughed. "When she found out we were having a *boppli*, you wouldn't have seen a happier more delighted woman. I've never seen her glow so much. Her face was lit up every day, and for it to end like that.…"

"It's hard to understand why things happen sometimes."

"She and my *boppli bu* were taken from me so quickly." He couldn't stop the tears and wiped them away with the back of his hand.

Sarah reached over and gave his hand a squeeze. He looked into her eyes and saw her sympathetic face, and the warmth and compassion coming from her comforted him.

"Do you have children, Sarah?"

"Thomas and I were never able to have any."

"Then you might know how Veronica felt."

"I do. More than you know. We're to have one, though, at the end of the year."

He leaned forward. "You're having a *boppli*? That's some *gut* news. Your husband must be overwhelmed with happiness."

"He was when he heard. He couldn't stop smiling for weeks when he learned the news, but now…"

He cut across her, "Now we know each other's stories…"

It was her turn to interrupt. "We each have one when we get to our ages."

He nodded. "I guess that's true. It's nice to learn more about one of Ruth's daughters."

"How does it make you feel when these women in the community bring you pies?"

"I feel horrible–just horrible. For them as well as myself. What do I say to them without upsetting them? How do I let them know I'm not interested?"

"There's only one way. You'll have to tell them. They'll be upset, but they'll get over it."

He sighed. "I don't want to hurt anyone's feelings."

"If you don't tell them, you'll only hurt them further along, and by then they might have wasted a lot of time on you."

"You're right, Sarah."

"I know I am. They could've been baking pies for another man."

He knew she was joking with that last comment, but what she said was true. He'd have to find the courage to be forthright with these women. He'd married the love of his life and she was all that he'd ever need.

"Perhaps, when you're letting them down gently, don't tell them how much in love with your wife you were. It'll touch their hearts and they'll hope that one day you'll love them like you once loved her."

He raised his eyebrows. "Is that how women think?" He watched Sarah nod. "How about you tell them for me, then?"

She burst out laughing. "I'm afraid that's something you'll have to do for yourself. If I could help you I would."

He sighed. "I know. I'll have to do it. So, you're selling the house for Ruth after the work is done?"

"That's the plan so far. My *mudder* wants to move in with me. Oh wait—she's already moved in with me."

"That'll be a blessing, having your *mudder* so close. She'll be a help with the *boppli.*"

"*Jah,* it will be different."

"You're blessed to still have your *mudder* around."

"You don't have any *familye?*"

"It's just me. Of course, Veronica's *familye* is here, but with her gone, and the baby too, I don't see them very often. Mine disowned me when I joined the Amish back when I was nineteen. I met

44

and married Veronica two years after that."

"*Ach,* that's a surprise. I thought King was an Amish name. And then there's your first name."

"I guess it is. I've known some people with the last name of King in the community, but I'm no relation. Isaac is my middle name. My first name is Warwick, but when I joined the community, I took on my middle name. It was a fresh start for a new life."

"That's interesting. And you've had no contact with your *familye?* "

"The community is my *familye.* It's best to stay separate."

Sarah nodded.

"So will you be selling the horse and buggy?"

"*Jah. Mamm* mentioned you might be interested in the horse."

He chuckled. "I took Ruth to the auction and we chose the horse together. He's a fine horse."

"I'm sure *Mamm* would like you to have the horse and buggy. She'll have no need of them."

"*Nee.* I can't have that."

"Why not? Don't answer that now. We can wait until the time comes, and then we'll sort things out."

"That sounds like a reasonable idea."

When Isaac had finished the last couple sips of his coffee, it was time to go.

"When can you get the quotes for the materials and start work on the place?"

"How soon would you like me to start?"

"I just have to sort the finances out with my *mudder* after I know how much everything will be."

"I'll try to have a price worked out for you by the end of the day."

"That would be *wunderbaar, denke.*"

Isaac left the house feeling like he'd made a friend. He hadn't talked to anybody about Veronica until now, because everybody here knew how she'd died. It had felt good to talk about his wife.

Chapter 6

Therefore know that the Lord your God,
He is God, the faithful God who keeps
covenant and mercy for a thousand generations
with those who love Him and keep His
commandments;
Deuteronomy 7:9

That afternoon, Isaac returned to Ruth's house. Sarah had been to town to get a large sum of money out of the bank for him to get started. It wouldn't be enough for everything, she thought, but she was more than certain it would allow him to buy some building materials.

He handed her three sheets of paper and she looked down at all the scribbles.

"And what's this?" she asked when she looked back up at him.

"It's the list of things that need to be done; along with what everything will cost."

She handed it back to him. "It's all gobbledygook

to me. Can you just give it to me straight? What will it cost?"

"It'll be three thousand two hundred dollars. That's the estimate."

"To do everything?"

He nodded.

"Are you certain?"

"So far I am, unless something else crops up that'll need to be done."

"I thought it would be much more."

"It would be, but remember, Ruth's not paying for labor only for materials. And I get a good discount because I buy from the same suppliers all the time. They look after me."

"I can give you the money right now. I went to the bank today."

"I won't need it all at once."

"Come inside and I'll get it for you."

He followed her inside and they both looked out the window by the front door when they heard a buggy.

"Ach nee! It's Wilma Hershberger," Isaac said.

"Is she a friend of my *mudder's?*"

"*Nee,* but for the purposes of her visit she'll most likely pretend to be. I'm sorry to involve you in all this."

"In all what?"

"Never mind."

Seeing the look of fear in Isaac's green eyes, Sarah guessed, "She's one of the pie ladies?"

He nodded.

"What should I do?"

"She will have seen my buggy here and she'll try to find out all about you to see if you're competition for her."

"Competition for what?"

"Competition for me."

Sarah burst out laughing.

He smiled. "Don't be like that. These women are serious in their attempts to marry me."

Sarah did her best to stifle her giggles. "Oh, I don't doubt that. Sorry to sound so shocked. What do you want me to do? I can't ask her to leave. I'll have to invite her inside."

"Jah. I'll stay for a few minutes and then make an excuse to leave. If I might ask you, though, not to let on I'll be working on the *haus* here for the next few weeks? Otherwise, she'll be here every day and I won't get any work done."

"I can do that."

"Denke."

"I'll get you that money."

By the time Sarah got the money, Wilma had tied up her horse and was already knocking on the door.

Sarah opened the door with Isaac close behind her. Isaac introduced the two women and then promptly announced he was just leaving. He didn't stay a few moments to be polite, even though he'd said he would.

"Come in, Wilma. Would you like a cup of hot tea?" Sarah asked.

"Jah, denke. I'd like that very much. It's so nice to finally meet you. I think I met you before, last time you visited. Many years ago I think that was."

"Jah, I think so. Take a seat in the living room and I'll be right out as soon as I put the pot on the

stove."

Wilma ignored Sarah's instructions and followed her into the kitchen and sat herself down at the kitchen table.

"You know my *mudder* well?" Sarah asked while filling the pot with water.

"*Jah,* extremely well. She said she was going to live with one of her *dochder's,* so is that you?"

"*Jah,* I've come back here to gather a few of her things and while I'm here, she's at my place." Sarah lit the stove, and placed the pot on the burner.

"Have you just met Isaac?"

"I think I met Isaac last time I was here, but neither of us can remember exactly."

"And are you married?"

"I'm widowed."

She noticed that Wilma stiffened.

"It's only just happened. The funeral was just a few days ago."

"I'm sorry to hear that."

Sarah nodded. *"Denke.* I want nothing more to go home and look after my poor old *mudder,"* she said, so Wilma wouldn't think she were romantically interested in Isaac. "And are you married, Wilma?" Sarah already knew the answer.

"Nee. I was married briefly, but he died a year into our marriage. That was ten years ago."

"Ach, ten years ago?"

Wilma nodded.

Sarah's heart went out to the young woman. "Then we both know the pain of losing husbands."

"Jah, only my pain has got easier over time, but I guess yours is still quite raw."

"It is. Everyone says it gets easier. I hope that's true for me."

"It will be." Wilma smiled at her. "Do you get lonely?"

The truth was she had been lonely already in the past two years once the illness had taken ahold of her husband. It was hard to watch him slipping away from her. She missed how their relationship had been when he'd been healthy. "I haven't had a chance for loneliness. My *mudder* showed up the day of the funeral and now here I am. I don't think

I'll be lonely with *Mamm* living with me."

Right now, loneliness sounded good to Sarah. She hadn't even had a chance to be alone and reflect upon what life without Thomas would mean. Soon, she'd go back home and then her baby would arrive while her mother would be expecting her to organize the building of the *grossdaddi haus.* All she wanted was to be alone and absorb the reality of what life would be like now that Thomas was gone, and prepare for the baby soon to be born.

"Are you all right, Sarah?"

"Jah, why?"

"The pot is boiling."

Then Sarah heard the water furiously bubbling. She jumped up, took the pot off the stove and proceeded to make the tea.

"Do you live close by?" Sarah asked when she'd sat back down with two full teacups. Wilma wasn't an unattractive woman and she seemed quite nice and not at all a woman that a man would normally want to avoid. She had a full face with warm brown eyes, and a few wisps of sandy blonde hair were poking out from the front of her prayer *kapp.*

Wilma picked up her teacup. *"Denke.* I don't live that far. Can I ask what Isaac King was doing here?"

"Isaac was… giving me a message to give to my *mudder."*

"Jah, they were *gut* friends. Your *mudder* will be greatly missed. She's been helpful to so many."

Again, Sarah wondered whether they were speaking about the same person. If she hadn't been to her mother's house before, she would be convinced she was in someone else's house—that would be the only thing that would make sense. The way in which Wilma and Isaac had described her mother sounded nothing at all like her perception of *Mamm.* "Exactly how has she been helpful?"

"In many ways." Wilma took a sip of tea. "She's always there whenever anyone needs anything. She's the person people turn to first if they don't want to talk with the bishop about things."

"I see." Sarah looked down at her tea and thought she'd better start drinking before it went cold.

"And are your folks from around here, Wilma?"

Wilma nodded. "They're all in this community. I have five brothers and two sisters and they all have at least three *kinner.* I'm the only one with no *kinner* and no spouse."

"You have a lot of nieces and nephews?"

"Jah, and that's nice, but it's not the same. I love them, of course, I do. It's nearly like having my own, but in my heart, I crave to have my own."

"I know how you feel."

"You do?"

Sarah nodded and realized she'd have to change the subject. If Wilma found out she was pregnant, she would pretend to be pleased for her, but it would be another blow to her. All too well, Sarah had been in the position of hearing someone's good news of an impending birth—she would smile on the outside while on the inside thinking, *'Why not me?'*

Sarah jumped up. "I think *Mamm* has some cookies in the pantry."

"Nee, don't bother finding them for me. I'm

watching my weight."

"Are you certain?"

Wilma nodded.

Sarah slowly slid back into the chair trying to think what they could talk about to keep the conversation from returning to Isaac. "What a pretty color your dress is."

"*Denke.* I made it just last week. I thought it might be too dark for me, but many people have said they like it." She took another sip of tea. "How long will you be staying here for?"

"Maybe a few weeks."

"It won't take a few weeks to gather your *mudder*'s things, will it?"

"*Nee,* but my *mudder* wants me to talk with some realtors about selling the *haus.* She said I must stay here and rest for a few weeks before I call one."

"That's a strange thing."

"I think a rest is what I need."

"I don't doubt that you do. I didn't mean it like that. Couldn't you have rested and then come here? It seems an odd thing that you're here and your *mudder* is there."

A perfect arrangement, Sarah thought before she blinked rapidly under Wilma's steely gaze.

Did Wilma have an idea that Isaac would be there working every day for the next few weeks. Was Wilma 'fishing' for information? There'd be nothing worse than having Wilma under her feet every day, as well as having Isaac trying to work. She had to think of something to say and think fast. "You see, Wilma, my *mudder* and I had a disagreement. I thought it best to put some distance between us, so I came here." It wasn't a lie. Her mother and she had disagreements all the time.

"I can't imagine what you'd have a disagreement about."

"Sometimes *familye* is like that. We most often hurt the ones we're closest with."

"I guess that's true," Wilma agreed.

Sarah continued, "So, that's why I'm here for a few weeks, and to get used to my husband being gone. To do that, I need time alone. I can't be alone at home now that my *mudder* is at my *haus*. Do you see?"

"I understand completely. Before I go, I'll write down my address so you can visit me while you're here. If you get lonely, you can come see me. I won't bother you since you came here to be alone."

Perfect! "That would be *wunderbaar, denke.*"

"You will be coming to the meeting on Sunday, won't you?"

"I wouldn't miss it. Where will it be?"

"It's at my *bruder's haus.* I'll write down that address for you too, unless you'd like me to stop by and take you there? I don't mind at all. It's not that much out of my way."

"Nee denke. It's kind of you to offer, but it's *gut* for the horse to get some exercise."

"Jah, of course."

When Wilma left, Sarah realized she had no idea when Isaac would be commencing work. She hoped it would be the very next morning.

Chapter 7

And Jesus, when he was baptized,
went up straightway out of the water:
and, lo, the heavens were opened unto him,
and he saw the Spirit of God descending
like a dove, and lighting upon him:
Matthew 3:16

"*D*enke for getting me out of an awkward situation yesterday," Isaac said gruffly, hugging a basket under his arm.

She stepped back to let him inside her mother's house. "*Gute mariye* to you too," Sarah said with a giggle.

Isaac laughed. "I'm sorry. *Gute mariye!* I was just nervous for you when I left you alone with Wilma."

"I told her I came here to be alone and have a rest for a time. I didn't mention anything at all about you doing work on the place."

"*Gut. Denke* for doing that."

"You're welcome. She's a very nice lady."

"They all are. Will you be using the kitchen today?"

"I figure I'll have to if I want to eat."

"Cook today for tomorrow, then, because I'll need to move on to some work in the kitchen tomorrow. The stove will need to be moved so I can replace those missing and cracked tiles behind it."

"Okay. Where will you start today?"

"The ceiling in the living room. I know that the leak on the roof was fixed six months ago, but the cosmetic work was left undone."

"How do you know about the leak?"

"I fixed the roof some time ago. Your *mudder* wouldn't let me paint the ceiling. I'm glad she's reconsidered. I'll have to clean it up and then repaint it."

"Okay. Have you had something to eat already?"

"I have. Don't mind me—just pretend I'm not here. I've brought my own *kaffe* and my own food for the day." He nodded at the basket under his arm.

"*Nee,* you didn't need to do that."

He laughed. "I don't want you fussing around me."

"Okay. Well, bring it through to the kitchen." She went in to fix herself some eggs for breakfast. Then she intended to cook up the meat she had bought the day before. That would be enough meat to last for a few days, she figured.

"I'll get started," he said as he headed out of the kitchen.

"Okay. Let me know if you need anything."

He didn't answer.

She suddenly felt little movements in her belly, like butterfly wings. That was just how her friend had described feeling the first kicks of her baby. She pressed her hands against her stomach. She'd felt the same sensations a few weeks ago, but hadn't known whether they were just in her imagination. Now they were stronger, and she knew that she was feeling her baby moving around. As pleased as she was, she couldn't help being disappointed that Thomas wasn't around to share her joy.

* * *

Later in the day, she noticed Isaac sitting on the sun-drenched porch, just where she'd intended on drinking her meadow tea.

"Mind if I join you?" she asked with tea in hand.

"It's your place. Well, your *mudder's.*" He pointed to the chair next to him and she sat down.

"It's a beautiful day," Sarah said, squinting as she looked up toward the sun.

"It sure is. The sun is warm, but not burning hot. I like the springtime on days like this."

"Me too." She took a sip of tea while she resisted asking him if she could fix him something to eat. She glanced down by his feet and saw the sandwiches he'd talked about earlier.

Isaac stared at the sandwiches by his feet, picked up his container and offered one to Sarah.

"What are they?" She peered at them.

"They're salted beef."

She frowned. *"Nee denke.* Did you cook that yourself?"

"I did. I'm quite a *gut* cook."

Sarah giggled. "I'll have to take your word for

that."

It is nice to have the company of a woman, Isaac thought. And with Sarah being married there was no threat that she'd become interested in him and turn her hand to baking. *"Nee* you don't."

She fixed her blue eyes on him. "What do you mean?"

"Tomorrow I'll cook you dinner and bring it over. It's the least I can do since you won't be able to use your stove. I can't have you starve. Ruth might never forgive me."

"Nee, you can't go to all that trouble when you're already working so hard."

"I like cooking. It's not work to me and besides, we both have to eat."

"I guess that'll save me cooking."

"Then it's settled. You'll taste my cooking and then you'll know that men can cook as good as women."

"I never doubted it."

He found himself laughing and relaxing for the first time in quite a while.

"What does your husband do?"

When she took a while to answer, Isaac figured they might be having marital problems and that's why she'd come there alone. "You don't have to answer that. I was just trying to make conversation to find out a little more about you since you're Ruth's *dochder.*"

"There's not much to tell. One thing I can tell you is that you seem to get along better with my *mudder* than I do." Sarah giggled.

"Nee!" he stared at her face and saw that it was true—she wasn't joking. "I can't understand that. She seems so easy to get along with."

"Maybe it's me then."

He frowned. "I can't think that it would be either of you."

"You're far too kind."

"No one can ever be too kind."

"We're harshest sometimes with those we love, maybe because we know they'll never leave us," she said.

"That's true. They're stuck with us." He thought

64

back to his siblings who'd been harsh with his decision about joining the Amish.

"Are you talking about how you had to leave your family to join us?"

He nodded. "It wasn't even a hard decision. I knew I had to do the right thing in the sight of *Gott.*"

"They wouldn't have been able to understand your choice."

"Nee. They didn't. That was years ago and I've not heard a word from any of them since."

"It might be best that way."

"You're most likely right, but it's been harder on me since my wife died."

Ruth's horse whinnied from the paddock at another horse who was pulling a buggy on a distant road.

"What do you like about my *mudder's* horse?"

"He takes direction well. He's been well trained and knows what to do. And he's a fine looking horse too. Ruth's looked after him well."

"She told me she had a neighbor boy feeding

him while she was gone. I must find him and tell him that I'm here now."

"That'll be the Fullers." He pointed to the house.

"Denke. I should've done that yesterday, but I thought I'd see the boy around. It looks like I missed him today."

"One of the boys would've come and fed the horse before *schul.* It could've been at five or six in the morning."

"That would've been way too early for me."

"Did I wake you too early?"

"Nee. Seven is fine. I was awake and just about to make breakfast."

"I'll bring breakfast for us tomorrow. I don't want the stove to be hot because I'll have to move it out of the way to do those repairs in the tiles behind it."

"Okay. So, you'll bring breakfast and dinner?"

"Jah, and the midday meal too."

"I don't know if I can let you do all of that."

"You can. And I won't hear another word about it."

When Sarah laughed, Isaac watched her and had the same feeling he used to have when he listened to his late wife laugh. It was nice to hear that sound again while the sun warmed him. He reached for his last sandwich while he realized he'd have to get to the store to buy food before it shut.

"I'll finish at four today."

"Okay."

When Sarah smiled at him he was pleased. "You know, you're a lot like your *mudder.*"

Sarah laughed again. "No one has said that to me—ever."

"You are."

"How do you figure that?"

"She's a *gut* listener and you've got that same kind self-assuredness as her." Now it was his turn to laugh. "I'm not even certain if self-assuredness is a real word, but you both have this kind of calmness about you as though everything will be okay."

When she seemed nervous and touched the strings of her prayer *kapp,* he wondered if he were being too familiar with a married woman. "I didn't mean to offend you. I just mean that I enjoy your company." Was he making things worse? He studied her to see if he had offended her in any way.

She smiled. "I enjoy yours too. And I'm determined to make the most of my time away from home. I know when I get back, my *mudder* will want to build the *grossdaddi haus* immediately."

"Is your husband able to help with that or is he still not well enough?"

"He won't be able to help, but knowing my *mudder,* she would've already found someone who'll be able to build it. She's not one for letting the grass grow under her feet. That's why I was surprised to see her *haus* in this state."

"Grief can do strange things to a person."

"My *vadder's* been gone for a few years."

"*Jah,* but she's been living here. She might not have wanted to change anything because if she did, that would mean she was doing things without him."

"I see. That makes sense. That's why she left and sent me back to do the repairs and arrange to sell the *haus.*"

He nodded. "We don't always speak what's in our minds and our hearts; not even to those closest."

"I guess that's true."

"I know it is." He bit into his sandwich and chewed thoughtfully. When he'd swallowed, he said, "I haven't changed a thing in my home since Veronica's been gone."

As Sarah listened to him speak, she thought back to her home. She hadn't even considered changing anything, let alone throwing out any of Thomas' things. It was silly to be sentimental over possessions; one day she might give his things to the charity store, but there was plenty of time for that.

Chapter 8

The Lord is my strength and my shield;
my heart trusted in him, and I am helped:
therefore my heart greatly rejoiceth;
and with my song will I praise him.
Psalm 28:7

When Sarah finished her tea, they sat talking for some time.

"I'll leave you to it, then," she finally said, thinking he'd better get back to work. She stood up and, as he had his mouth full, he gave a small wave and nodded his head.

She walked back into the house to cook the dinner.

When Isaac went back to work, Sarah made certain she stayed out of his way. Eventually he'd find out she was widowed and she didn't want to be on his list of women that he avoided. She wanted to remain friends with him. It would've been best if she'd told him upfront, but she had tried a couple of times. Sarah laughed to herself at the thought of him thinking she was a pie lady when she first knocked on his door.

A few hours later, Isaac called out to her letting her know that he was going. Sarah was upstairs cleaning the bedrooms.

She opened the bedroom window and stuck her head out to wave. "Bye, Isaac."

He looked up at her. "I'll see you bright and early tomorrow."

"Okay." She watched him get into the buggy and drive away from the house.

It was strange to be in the house without her mother or father. She headed down to the kitchen for an early dinner. Just as she sat down, there was a knock on the door. She opened it to see Isaac.

"I forgot it was Sunday tomorrow, so it'll be Monday before I'll be here again. You'll have use of your stove for another day."

"*Jah,* I forgot what day it was too. So Monday, you'll be bringing breakfast and dinner?"

When he hesitated, she added, "I'm holding you

to it."

He laughed. "Monday, I'll bring both breakfast and dinner."

"Gut!"

"Will you be coming to our meetings while you're here?"

"I will. Wilma gave me the address and told me it was at her *bruder's haus.*"

"That's right."

"I'll be there. Wilma gave me the directions."

"I look forward to seeing you."

* * *

Sarah sat through the church service barely listening to what was being said. She'd met two of her mother's friends and they'd insisted that she sit with them. As the bishop spoke, Sarah was too busy wondering which of the ladies were married and which ones were the ones chasing Isaac. Wilma was sitting two rows in front of her and there was no guessing why Wilma's head was constantly tilted to the left, where Isaac sat amongst the men. There was another lady sitting in the row in front of Wilma, and she seemed to be glancing in his direction as well.

After the meeting was over, Sarah was at the refreshments table in the yard when she looked across to see Isaac engrossed in a conversation with another man. The man nodded toward Sarah, and Sarah looked away but not before she noticed out of the corner of her eye that Isaac turned to look at her. She resumed deciding which foods to put on her plate.

"Mrs. Hersler."

Sarah turned around to see Isaac. "We're being formal? Mr. King, it's nice to see you again."

"I heard something about you."

Sarah gave a small laugh when she figured he'd found out the truth. She hoped he didn't mind her not telling him upfront. "News doesn't take long to travel around here. What did you hear?"

"I heard that you buried your husband only weeks ago."

"That's correct. I'm sorry I misled you. I didn't mean to. I started to tell you a couple of times when we first met, and each time I was interrupted and the moment passed. We were looking at the house repairs then. After that, I didn't want you to think that I was another widow trying to marry you."

Isaac looked thoughtful. "I sound like an ogre, and I'm not."

She was pleased that he didn't seem to mind her keeping that information from him.

"If I'd told you right away that I was widowed, would you have talked so openly with me?" Sarah asked.

"Probably not, but maybe I would've when I found out you were Ruth's *dochder* and the reason you were here." He shook his head. "I have to rethink my actions."

"You're not the only one. I'm truly sorry to mislead you in the way that I did."

"And I'm sorry to have caused you to do it. It seems we're both even."

"Shall we call a truce, then?"

"I didn't know we were fighting," he said with a cheeky grin.

She laughed again.

"What is it that you have to tell me, Sarah? Is there anything else I should know? You haven't replaced me as a builder have you?"

"Nee, I haven't and if I wanted to, my *mudder* wouldn't let me. You're quite safe. I have no secrets now."

"Gut! Neither do I. You know them all," he said with a lopsided smile.

Sarah noticed two women coming from different directions heading towards them. She guessed they were coming to talk with Isaac and not herself. "Don't turn around now, but there are two women heading this way looking directly at you."

The corners of his mouth turned down. "The story of my life lately."

"Can I help in any way?"

He sighed. "I think I'm beyond help, Sarah."

They exchanged smiles.

"I'll see you tomorrow morning?" Sarah asked.

"I'll be there, bright and early."

Sarah gave both ladies a smile as they were just about level with Isaac. She looked around for the bishop to say hello. She'd met him before, but thought he might not remember who she was without her mother nearby.

Chapter 9

Also I say unto you,
Whosoever shall confess me before men,
him shall the Son of man also confess before the
angels of God:
Luke 12:8

The next morning, just as Sarah started drinking a cup of hot tea, she heard a horse heading to the house. She looked out the window to see Isaac in his wagon. How much could he do today in the rain?

She walked outside under the cover of the porch. "Hello."

"Hi," he said as he jumped down from the wagon.

"Can you do much work today?"

"*Jah,* It's mostly inside work."

"You didn't forget breakfast, did you?"

"*Nee, denke.* I've already eaten."

"We had an arrangement," she said with a pretend frown.

He laughed. "I've got it. I didn't forget." He picked up a basket out of the back of the wagon and headed toward her.

"I wouldn't mind a cup of *kaffe*."

"Done."

They sat in the kitchen as the rain poured down. They ate warm pancakes with maple syrup.

"I'm sorry that they aren't hot."

"It doesn't matter. They are very tasty."

He drained the last of his coffee. "I'll start in the barn. I've got some wood to cut."

"Then you have to move the stove?"

"Jah, I'll move on to the kitchen later in the morning."

As he stood up from the table, Sarah stood and gathered the dishes to wash. Soon, he was outside heading to the barn. She watched him from the kitchen window. There was something about the man that she liked. No wonder the women were after him. She could fully understand how they found his quiet confidence and ready smile appealing.

Feeling a sudden desire for pickles, she looked in her mother's pantry hoping she kept a jar in there. *Denke, Gott—pickles.* She reached for the jar knowing she must be having a craving. She'd never been fond of pickles at all. The lid was stuck on hard. Try as she might, she couldn't open it. There was only one thing to do. She headed to the door and looked out. It had stopped raining. While Isaac was there she could make use of him, she decided. She carefully navigated her way between the puddles that the last downpour had caused.

"Isaac," Sarah called out from the door of the barn.

"Over here."

She looked in to see him in an unused stall just about to saw a piece of wood. "There you are."

He looked up at her and then rose to his feet. "What can I do for you?"

She handed him the pickle jar. "I can't get this jar off. I mean, lid off. I can't get the lid off the jar."

Without saying a word, he took the jar and twisted the lid, and then handed it back to her.

"Oh, that looked easy."

"It was easy for me."

"Well, I'll have to work on my muscle strength." Just as she said that, the rain poured down. "*Nee!* That can't be rain! It didn't even look like rain when I walked into the barn."

"According to the forecast it'll be raining on and off all day."

"*Ach!*"

They both walked to the barn door and looked out at the sky, which was dark with clouds.

"Well it's certainly raining now," Sarah said.

"Don't go back in there, stay here a while and wait out the rain."

"I had no intention of going back in there. I don't want to risk falling."

"I've got a couple of pieces of wood to saw and then I'll stop for a while."

"I'll watch." She sat on a bale of hay as she ate pickles straight from the jar.

When he was done sawing, he explained what he was going to do with the wood. "Didn't I feed you enough?" he asked when he saw her eating the pickles.

She giggled. "I just need some pickles. I was going to have them with tomato sauce. That was what I was craving, but now I just have to settle for the pickles."

"I can go over and get it for you."

"Nee, the rain's too heavy."

He laughed. "It's only water."

"I can't have you do that. You'll get soaked through and then catch a cold. I can't have that."

"Why don't you eat some of the sandwiches I made? They've got tomato on them and might quell your cravings a little bit."

"I can't do that."

"You can. I'm not that hungry. You can find me something to eat later when the rain stops. Come on. I can't have you going hungry. I've got the lunch in the wagon."

Sarah glanced at the wagon that was in the undercover area of the barn.

"Care for some bacon and tomato sandwiches

with relish?"

She laughed. "It sounds an interesting combination."

"That's a strange comment coming from a woman who eats pickles straight from the jar. Anyway, don't knock something until you try it." He gave her a smile and headed to his wagon. "Come on, I'll sit with you."

"Okay."

Sarah climbed up into the wagon and sat next to Isaac. He opened a packet of the sandwiches and handed them to her.

"Just as well, I'm hungry."

"Just try it," he urged her.

She bit into the sandwich. When she swallowed, she said, "It's not horrible."

He laughed. "I'll take that as a good thing. And I guess I'll have some, too. You're making me hungry."

Knowing that they were in for a long day, she asked, "Where did you grow up."

"Not far from here. I think I told you about my

family and how they disowned me when I joined the Amish."

"Yes you did tell me, and I was sorry to hear that."

"It was probably for the best."

"Do you feel lonely?"

"Nee. I've got many friends within the community. Ruth was like my *mudder,* and that's why I was bit surprised that she left without a word."

"Maybe she didn't intend to stay but when she got to my place the thought of returning was too much for her. She's like that. She'd never say she hadn't planned something."

"Jah, I can see her being like that. Ruth's a forthright woman and doesn't want to be seen as someone who would change her mind or not be certain about something."

"That's what she's like—exactly."

"And what about you?"

"Me?"

He nodded.

"I had many brothers and sisters and my husband, as you know has just died. He was sick for a long time. The last few weeks he couldn't get out of bed."

"That must've been hard on you."

"It was hard for me when he left me alone."

"I know what that's like, when someone you love leaves you to be with *Gott*. Even though we know we'll see them again, it's lonely without them."

"Did you know my *mudder* arrived the day of my husband's funeral—after it was over?"

"Do you think she meant to make it for the funeral?"

"It's hard to say, but she arrived and said that now that I don't have to look after Thomas anymore I can look after her."

"And she wants a *grossdaddi haus* built, you said?"

"*Jah.* She said she doesn't want to be bothered by crying."

"You intend to do a lot of crying?"

Sarah laughed. "My *mudder* says she has had

86

enough of raising *kinner*. And she's got enough *grosskin*. She didn't know I was expecting when she arrived. She wasn't too happy about it when I told her. It threw out her plans of living in my *haus*."

"You sound like you haven't always gotten along with Ruth."

Sarah didn't want to make it sound like she was an unreasonable person. "We don't always see eye-to-eye about things. It would've been nice if she'd been happy for me, though, that I am having a *boppli*."

"I'm sure she is. She was most likely shocked since that was something she wouldn't have expected to hear."

"I guess so."

"I'm so happy for you; that's such a blessing," he said. "*Gott* took Thomas home, but He blessed you with a child to keep you from being lonely."

Tears came to Sarah's eyes as he spoke. "You're right. He blessed me with something I've always wanted—a *boppli*."

"I guess it's bittersweet."

"It is, exactly, because my husband won't see his child come into the world. He won't be around to watch the *boppli* grow. And my *boppli* won't have a *daed,* but it'll do me no good to dwell on that kind of thinking. There are many worse off than I."

He shook his head. "You've been mightily blessed. Don't question what *Gott* has put into place. We might never know the reasons for things that happen. And you're right, as bad as things get there are always people who are much worse off."

"Denke, you've made me feel so much better."

"That's what friends are for." He took her hand and squeezed it. For a brief moment they stared into each other's eyes before he pulled his hand away.

It wasn't a moment of romance, it was a moment of appreciation for one another — a meeting of the minds.

He smiled as he passed her another sandwich. "Here, eat up."

The rain had stopped at the same time they had run out of sandwiches.

"I don't hear any rain," Sarah said.

"Just as well because you've eaten all my sandwiches. Does that mean you liked them after all?"

"They were quite passable."

He smiled at her. "I have to get back to work."

"Don't forget you said you'd bring the evening meal over tonight because I won't have the stove."

"I wouldn't be able to forget something like that. And now I know you'll be looking forward to the food because you liked my sandwiches so much."

Sarah laughed as she climbed down from the wagon. "I'll leave that for you to sort out."

She walked carefully back to the house, making sure she didn't slip on the wet ground.

Isaac didn't tell Sarah, but he'd already made a lamb stew with plenty of vegetables. That was his favourite and he hoped she would like it too. He had been surprised when she'd first told him that she was expecting a child, given her age. And, at that time, he hadn't known that she had been widowed.

Chapter 10

But as for me, I will walk in mine integrity:
redeem me, and be merciful unto me.
Psalm 26:11

Isaac spent the next two hours cutting wood to size, matching the measurements that he'd taken the day before. When he was done, he knocked on the door.

"Come in," she said, stepping back when she saw him at the front door.

"Have you eaten all the pickles yet?"

"Not yet. I've left some for you."

"How kind. Now, I have to do that work in the kitchen."

"Well, you know the way. I've moved everything but the stove for you."

"Denke."

"I'll keep out of your way," she called after him.

She sat down and took up some knitting that she'd found in her mother's room. *Mamm* had been in the middle of knitting some kind of a blanket, but she'd left it there when she traveled to Sarah's home.

When it was getting dark, Isaac emerged from the kitchen.

"Are you ready for dinner?" he asked.

"I am. Do you have to go home and get it?"

"I do. I've made you a lamb and vegetable stew."

"Denke. That sounds lovely. I've worked up quite an appetite with all this knitting."

"I'll go home and fetch it."

"I'll have to go to the store tomorrow. I'm running low on a few things. Just as well you're bringing the dinner over."

"You're running low on pickles?" he asked with a chuckle.

"Amongst other things."

"Would you like me to go for you?"

"Nee, there's no need. I can still do things for myself."

He smiled. "I didn't think that you couldn't but sometimes it's nice to have other people do things for us."

"I'm fine."

"I'll only be an hour."

They smiled at one another before he headed to his wagon.

* * *

As Isaac drove home, he admitted to himself that he liked Sarah as more than a friend because he was so looking forward to seeing her that night. He hadn't gone looking for love again and neither had he expected it, but he was starting to feel as though he might be at risk of falling for Sarah.

He unhitched his horse as soon as he got home, and led him into the paddock. "Off you go, boy. I'll need you again soon, so don't get too comfortable."

The horse walked off with his tail swishing behind him.

Isaac looked down at his dusty clothes. He'd have to clean up before he did anything else. Rubbing his chin, he knew he'd have to shave and shower and look his best.

After his shower, Isaac pulled on black pants, and just when he was buttoning his white shirt, he heard a buggy. He looked out his bedroom window to see a buggy pulled by a bay horse. *Who could this be?*

He hurried downstairs and when he opened his door, he saw Elizabeth Shwartz walking toward him.

"Hello, Elizabeth."

"Hi, Isaac. I saw you yesterday with a lady and wondered if you have a visitor staying with you. I never got a chance to say hello to her."

"I don't have a visitor. The lady you saw is Ruth's *dochder.* She's not staying with me."

"Oh."

"Ruth has moved away." When Elizabeth stared at him without saying a word, Isaac added, "Ruth has moved to Lancaster County and her *dochder's* here tying up some lose ends."

"Ruth never said anything about leaving." She looked him up and down. "Are you going somewhere?"

"Jah, I am."

"Where?"

"I'm off to visit a friend."

"Can I go with you?"

He looked down at the boards on the porch thinking as quickly as he could. *"Nee,* you don't know the person I'm visiting."

"Would you be visiting Ruth's *dochder?"*

He was caught out. Now news would travel around the community that he was spending time with Sarah. And that would mean a lot more pies might be coming his way and many more visits. He couldn't lie, although the idea of telling a quick lie jumped into his mind as an easy way out. *"Jah,* I am."

"I'd like to meet her. Can't I come?"

Instead of answering her directly, he said, *"Gut!* Why don't you visit her tomorrow? I know for a fact she'll be there at twelve." Isaac had chosen that time because he intended to be elsewhere at twelve the next day. He'd see to it.

"I'll call and see her now."

"That wouldn't be a good idea."

"Why not? Do you want to visit her by yourself? Is that what this is about?"

"*Nee,* but I'm discussing some business things with her—things for Ruth." That wasn't a lie.

Elizabeth stared at him carefully. "I see."

He smiled at her. "I'm sorry. I can't stay and talk, I'm just about on my way out now."

She nodded. "I'll see you another time."

"*Jah,* another time." He was just grateful that she hadn't brought him a pie.

"I almost forgot. I have a pie for you. Ruth told me how much you like pies."

Isaac's jaw dropped open and before he could say anything, Elizabeth was back at her buggy. She lifted out the pie and headed toward him, proudly holding the pie in both hands.

"How kind and thoughtful of you, Elizabeth."

"I know it must be hard for a single man like you without a *fraa* to cook for you."

"I manage just fine, but *denke* for the pie."

When he took it out of her hands, she said, "It's a blackberry pie."

"Wunderbaar."

"I'll go now."

"Okay." He watched her from his doorway as she got into her buggy. She waved at him and then drove away.

He heaved a sigh and leaned against the doorpost. While he felt bad for these women, he didn't know what to say to them. How could he tell them he wasn't interested without hurting their feelings? Something told him that everyone in the community was convinced he needed a wife. And what was up with Ruth telling Elizabeth that he liked pies? He thought Ruth had been on his side this whole time. Ruth knew how he'd felt about Veronica and he'd shared with her his decision to remain as he was.

When Elizabeth's buggy was out of sight, he walked inside and placed the pie on the kitchen table. He'd figure out what to do with it later that night when he got home. He couldn't eat another pie and it wouldn't be nice of him to take it to Sarah's.

Isaac put the large saucepan, already filled with the stew, onto the stove to heat it. Once it was hot, he'd take the pot over to Sarah's place. He hoped she'd excuse him for not bringing a dessert. If he was a better cook, he could've tried his hand at some shoofly pies or some other traditional Amish sweet desserts. Since Veronica had gone, he'd taught himself to cook but had never gone past the basics for survival purposes only. Hopefully, Sarah would enjoy what had become his favorite dish.

When he rubbed his chin, he realized he still hadn't shaved. He left the dinner to heat in the saucepan while he headed back to the bathroom so he'd look as tidy as he possibly could.

Chapter 11

Ye are my witnesses, saith the Lord,
and my servant whom I have chosen:
that ye may know and believe me,
and understand that I am he:
before me there was no God formed,
neither shall there be after me.
Isaiah 43:10

Sarah took a shower and got ready for her dinner guest. It was nice to have a rest from cooking dinner. She liked being around Isaac, too. Although he'd seemed a little standoffish when she first knocked on his door, she could see now why so many women desired him.

The only thing she was determined to do was to make certain she didn't become one of those women. Any other woman in her position would be tempted to marry someone nice like Isaac. It would certainly make life easier to have a man around. Thomas had been sick for so long that she'd forgotten how it was to have a man who could do things such as repairs around the house.

Besides that, Isaac would be useful to help carry the burden of having her mother living beside her. It was good that Isaac got along so well with her mother.

She stopped and checked herself. What was she thinking? It was a ridiculous notion to think of another man so soon. She'd only just buried her husband a little over a week ago. It must be her pregnancy hormones making her feel vulnerable, she decided.

Maybe it was a good thing her mother had come to stay. Even though her mother claimed not to like children, at least there would be an extra pair of hands to help around the place when she really needed it.

"Denke, Gott," Sarah murmured as she got out of the shower. She could see how *Gott* was working. He'd taken Thomas away, blessed her with a baby, and placed her mother there so she would feel more settled through the birth and her baby's

first months. Even though she hadn't wanted her mother there at first, she now acknowledged that it might be a good idea.

Sarah pulled on a light blue dress and then tied her apron on over the top. She unbraided her hair, brushing it out before she braided it once more. After she had pinned her hair onto her head, she popped her prayer *kapp* on leaving the strings to hang down the sides of her neck as usual.

Her mother's house was strangely quiet. It was nice to get away from everything and everyone.

At the Sunday meeting just yesterday, she had gotten invitations to visit people but she had explained she had a limited time to oversee the building work before she placed her mother's house up for sale. There were many people who were amazed that her mother had made such a quick decision and left without a word. One of those people was the bishop.

The bishop told her he had been quite surprised by Ruth's sudden disappearance. Sarah had explained that it was a last-minute decision and explained that her mother had arrived on the day of her husband's funeral. It quietly amused Sarah to know that the bishop would assume that her mother had attended Thomas' funeral. The bishop accepted what she said with a nod of his head.

Sarah walked into the kitchen to see the state Isaac had left it in.

The stove was still away from its usual position while the replaced tiles behind it were left to dry. He'd also prepared all the cupboards for painting. The hinges and the handles were all off the doors that were spread along the floor on newspapers.

I don't think we'll be eating in here tonight.

She walked out of the kitchen and sat on the couch, waiting for Isaac to arrive and too tired to do anything else. There was always plenty of cleaning to be done, but Sarah excused herself from doing anything now since she'd just taken a shower. It was rare that she sat and did nothing, so she decided to soak in the peace and quiet.

* * *

Isaac got the stew out of the buggy and headed to the front door of Ruth's house.

"Hello," Isaac called out when he reached the door, because he had his hands full. When there was no answer, he peeked through the window and saw Sarah fast asleep on the couch. He chuckled quietly. He didn't want to wake her, so he balanced the stew on his knee with one hand and opened the door with the other. Once he was inside, he made his way into the kitchen and put the stew onto the kitchen table. When he walked back into the living room she was awake.

"You're here already? Was I asleep?" She yawned.

He laughed. "I hope you don't mind me coming in just now, but I saw you asleep and didn't want to startle you by knocking on the door. Was I too noisy in the kitchen?"

"Not at all. I'm glad I didn't miss out on dinner." Sarah gave a little laugh.

"I wouldn't let you do that."

"Well, where is it?" Sarah asked, pushing herself

to her feet.

"It's here, in the kitchen. Are you hungry now or do you want to wait a while?"

"I think we could eat now. But we might have to bring it out here and eat it sitting on the couch with our plates on our knees."

"It'll only be for two nights; I'll have the kitchen back to normal in no time. The stove will be okay to use tomorrow, but the paint on the cupboards will need time to dry. I'll paint them first thing tomorrow."

"Okay. We'll have to hope it's a nice warm day so everything dries quicker."

Together they walked into the kitchen.

Sarah took the lid off the saucepan and set it on the kitchen table. "This smells *gut!* And you did this by yourself?"

"Of course, I did. Who else would've done it for me?" She stared at him and he gave a crooked smile.

"Do I really need to name the people who could have cooked it for you?"

He laughed. *"Nee, denke!* I wouldn't have them cook for me. I did it myself."

"I'll get us some plates and cutlery. Can you carry it to the living room?"

Isaac picked up the pot, with the hot handles covered by tea towels.

Sarah said, "I hope you don't mind eating it on your lap."

"Nee. It goes down the same way." He placed the saucepan on the low wooden table in the living room.

Sarah served the stew onto two soup plates. "I should be letting you do this since you cooked it."

"I would've, but you just took over."

Sarah giggled. "Sit down and I'll hand you a plate."

She handed him a plate of food and then sat down with one herself. They both closed their eyes and said a silent prayer of thanks for the food.

Sarah opened her eyes and looked at Isaac.

"Go on. Try some."

She pushed her fork into a piece of meat and

popped it into her mouth. When she finished chewing, she said, "It's delicious."

"*Gut!*

She nodded. "Much better than I expected. You're full of surprises. I never thought you'd be able to cook this well."

"*Denke*—I think."

"What else can you do?"

"I told you before, I've had to do everything for myself for awhile with Veronica gone."

Isaac and Sarah sat and talked for hours, long after they'd finished the dinner.

"I'm sorry, I can't even offer you a cup of hot tea," Sarah said. "Since the stove isn't connected.

"We could light the fire."

She glanced at the fireplace. "I hope *Mamm* has it in good working order. I don't want the *haus* to fill with smoke."

"I drive past Ruth's *haus* most every day and in the winter the smoke was always coming out of the chimney—not the windows. I think we can risk it."

Sarah nodded. "I'll get some matches. It looks

like there's enough wood and kindling there."

"I'll build the fire."

"Okay." Sarah went to the kitchen to find the matches and a suitable pot to boil water in. When she came back, he had made a pile of wood and kindling. She handed him the matches and some firestarters.

Together they made a fire and boiled the water, talking and laughing all the while.

Chapter 12

*This is a faithful saying, and these things I will that
thou affirm constantly, that they which have believed
in God might be careful to maintain good works.
These things are good and profitable unto men.*
Titus 3:8

Ruth's house is completed.

"Well it's been a busy two months; what do
you think of it now?"

"I like it so much I might move here myself."

He laughed. "I don't know what your *mudder*
would say about that."

"She wouldn't like it, but she never likes anything
I do so what would be the difference?"

He laughed. "It's like you're speaking about
somebody else. I've never found Ruth to be like
that."

"It is possible I'm being too hard on her—a
small possibility, but I'll see if we can't get along

better when I go back home."

He laughed again. "You should do that. Now, on a different subject I've got somebody looking at the house this afternoon."

"Looking at it for what?"

"To buy."

"But I haven't even spoken to a realtor yet."

"You can do that today if you don't mind me showing the young couple through the house myself."

"Of course, I don't mind. Who are they?"

"A young couple from the community—they're getting married soon. They told me they've been looking for a house and I told them about Ruth's. They're quite interested. I'm sure they'll pay the going rate, whatever that might be, if they like it. They'll pay a fair price."

"I'm shocked that someone might be interested so soon. I thought it would be at least another six months to find a buyer." It struck Sarah then and there that she wanted to stay longer. She had enjoyed Isaac's company every day. They'd had at least one meal together daily since he'd started work on the house. The thought of going back home made her more than a little sad. Sarah glanced up at him and wondered if he felt the same.

"The sooner you get this place sold the sooner you can get back to your *mudder.*"

She shook her head and smiled while thinking what it would be like with her mother and herself under the same roof until the extension was built onto the house.

"I mean you can get back in enough time to settle in before the *boppli* is born."

"*Jah*, I guess I have to get things organized. I'm excited about the *boppli* coming, but I haven't had much time to think about it. There has been so much going on."

"You do have some organizing to do, but don't worry. I'm sure it will be easier than getting me and the house repairs systematized."

She laughed. "You did all that. *Denke* for everything. You've done a wonderful job. My *mudder* is blessed to have such a friend as you."

"I'm glad to have met you, Sarah. I really mean that."

"And I you."

He looked down at her and smiled.

"I suppose I better find a phone book and start calling a couple of realtors. I'll see if they can come by this morning before your friends arrive to see the *haus*."

"That would be best. I'll do some cleaning up while you're making your calls."

They went their separate ways.

When she came back inside from making the calls in the barn, she saw him sweeping the kitchen floor. "I can do that."

"So can I," he said without looking up.

"So I see. I've got two realtors coming here a little later on."

"*Gut.*"

"*Jah,* I guess if this young couple decides to buy the *haus*, *Mamm* will be pleased to have a quick sale."

"They're a nice young couple. Their names are

Ralene and Peter. I'm not sure if I mentioned that to you."

"Okay, Ralene and Peter. I'll try to remember that. Would you be able to stay for dinner tonight?"

"I'd like that."

"What time are your friends having a look through the house?"

"They said they'd be here at four o'clock. When are your realtors coming?"

"One is coming at eleven and the other one said one o'clock."

"That works out well. I'll just do a few last things around here and then I'll get out of your hair until just before Peter and Ralene get here."

After Isaac had gone, time passed slowly for Sarah. She spent the next few hours cleaning and polishing the house the best she could to make a good impression on the realtors.

Chapter 13

Now faith is the substance of things hoped for,
the evidence of things not seen.
Hebrews 11:1

Isaac arrived at the house fifteen minutes before the young couple was due to arrive.

"Why don't you take a walk while I show them around?" Isaac asked.

"Do you think that would be best?"

"Jah, they might feel more relaxed if you're not here. You might, too."

"Okay, I'll go for a walk."

"Before you go, what did the realtors say about the value?"

Sarah gave him the price range that both realtors had suggested.

"I'll come and find you when they're gone."

"Okay. And thanks again for doing this, Isaac."

"Why wouldn't I? It will work out well for everyone if Ralene and Peter buy Ruth's *haus.*"

Sarah walked away from the house, hoping that the young couple would find the house suitable. A prompt sale of the home would mean she could get on with her own life faster. She'd barely had enough time to adjust to Thomas being gone and the idea of having a baby.

When she was two paddocks over, she looked back at the house to see Isaac sitting on the porch.

* * *

Isaac sat on the porch waiting for his young friends to get there to look through the house. He was pleased that Sarah had enough confidence in him to leave things in his hands. In a way, he knew he was working against himself if Ralene and Peter bought the house quickly. He wanted Sarah to stay around as long as possible. In a few short weeks she'd become a good friend, and there weren't many people around that he was comfortable enough to talk with the way he could talk with Sarah.

He only hoped the feeling was mutual. When the time came for her to leave, he'd ask her to write to him. Perhaps he could even visit Sarah and Ruth in Lancaster County.

When he looked up, he saw Peter's horse and buggy heading toward him.

Peter was the first to jump out of the buggy, and Isaac headed to meet them.

"Is Ruth really selling?" Ralene asked, stepping down.

"She is. The *haus* needed a few things done to it, but now it's all finished and ready to be sold. I hope you'll both like it. I think it would suit you."

Ralene looked up at the house and when Peter stood beside her, Ralene said, "I think this will be just perfect."

Peter laughed. "Let's leave that decision until we've had a look inside."

"I can just tell," she insisted with a frown.

Isaac gave a little chuckle. "Come on, I'll show you through."

When they got into the living room, Isaac sat

down. "On second thought, I'll let you two have a little explore for yourselves and see what you think."

"Sounds good," Peter said before Ralene pulled him into another room.

Isaac knew that Ralene loved the place and she would most likely talk Peter into buying it.

The pair looked around the house for about fifteen minutes and then sat down opposite Isaac in the living room.

"We really like it," Ralene said.

"But it will depend on the price," Peter added.

When Isaac gave them the price range the two agents mentioned, Peter named a price that they'd be willing to pay.

"I'll let Ruth know. The ultimate decision is up to her. I'll let Sarah, her *dochder,* know and she can call Ruth."

"Good. How soon can you let us know?" Ralene asked.

"How does tomorrow sound?"

Peter said, "That would be good because we've

got some other places we want to look at."

"I'm sure we'll know by tomorrow," Isaac said.

Peter and Ralene looked lovingly into each other's eyes.

Isaac was transported back many years to the time when he and his wife had bought their house. They'd had great expectations of how life would be. They'd both taken for granted the notion that they'd be blessed with many children, but they were to find out that it wasn't in God's plan for them. Isaac hoped for the sake of this young couple that they wouldn't be disappointed in what they pictured for their future. If there was one thing Isaac had come to know about life, it was that life was unpredictable. Very often the things he'd planned had never worked out. He learned from experience that people make plans, but we have no power over those plans, as it is God who decides what's in everyone's future.

He looked back at the young couple who were still smiling—smitten with each other.

"I hope you'll both be very happy," he said,

wishing his own life had been different or that he could understand God's plans for him.

They looked at him, surprised, even a little amazed.

"*Denke,* Isaac, we'll be fine," Peter said.

Spoken with the confidence of the young, Isaac thought. "*Gott* willing."

* * *

Sarah had been walking in the top paddock when she saw Isaac heading toward her. There was now no buggy at the house and she knew that the young couple had been and gone. She stared at Isaac's face trying to get an inkling of how things had gone.

"How did it go?" she asked.

"Very good. They said they'd buy it at ten thousand under the top figure the realtors gave you."

"That sounds fair to me. I'll just have to clear it with my *mudder.* I'll call my friend and have her deliver the message to her."

"Don't you have a phone at your *haus?*"

"Nee, I normally borrow my friend's phone. Naomi is my friend and she lives next door. She got a phone connected a few years ago. Thomas and I always intended on getting one put in the barn, but there was always something to keep our attention from it. *Denke,* Isaac for arranging all this."

"I'm happy to do it."

"Mamm will be so pleased. Now she'll be away from me and the *boppli."*

Isaac laughed. "I thought she'd be happy to be in the middle of things."

"You don't know her as well as you think you do."

"I'm certain I know her quite well."

"Do you think you know me well too?"

"We've only just met." He stared at her and then his serious face broke into a smile. "Yes, I think I know you pretty well. I know you care enough about Ruth to drop everything and come here to get her *haus* sold for her."

Sarah raised her eyebrows. "I didn't have much of a choice about that. My *mudder* is very determined when she sets her mind to something."

Isaac laughed.

"She said there was no one else she wanted to do the work on her place but you."

"She said that?"

"Jah, she did. She insisted on it."

"Don't you have someone to build the *grossdaddi haus?"*

Sarah looked into his face and knew that he wouldn't need much persuading to do that job as well. It was too far away to be practical for him. Besides, as he'd done this job for her mother for nothing, he might insist on doing the next job for nothing, too, and Sarah just couldn't impose like that. "I'm certain I do." She knew many builders back home who'd be able to do the job.

He nodded looking away. Sarah could see disappointment etched into his features.

"I guess you'll be leaving soon, then?" he said when he looked back at her.

"I will. As soon as the contract paperwork is signed for the sale of *Mamm's haus.*"

He rubbed his chin. "I must delay that as much as I can." When she laughed, his eyes locked onto hers. "I'll miss you when you go, Sarah. I've enjoyed our time together."

"So have I."

"I like you."

"You only like me because I'm the only woman who hasn't brought you a cake."

"It was a pie."

"Ach jah, a pie."

He nodded, and with a twinkle in his eyes added, "I don't think pies have anything to do with it."

Sarah knew it wasn't a practical thing to do—to keep Isaac thinking there might be a chance of love in their future. She was tempted to let her emotions run away with her, but it would never work. In her heart she was pleased that he felt something for her too. The next thing she said was hard for her. She swallowed hard, before she said, "Perhaps you could give one of the pie ladies a chance?"

He narrowed his eyes. *"Nee,* never." After they laughed, he cleared his throat. "Might I visit both you and Ruth one day?"

"I'd like that, I'd really like that." She could very easily grow too fond of him, so it was just as well she was heading home soon.

"Denke."

* * *

Isaac turned down the dinner invitation that Sarah had extended him earlier that day. He didn't want to be at Ruth's house too often. Did Sarah have any inkling how he felt about her, or did she think he was merely joking when he admitted to liking her? He didn't want to think about her going home. There'd be a hole in his life. The funny thing was that they'd only known each other for a matter of weeks. Sarah was a delightful woman, and such women were in short supply—in his opinion.

Chapter 14

Draw me not away with the wicked,
and with the workers of iniquity,
which speak peace to their neighbours,
but mischief is in their hearts.
Psalm 28:3

Back at Sarah's house in Lancaster County

"There's only one person who can build it for me and that's Isaac King."

"*Mamm,* Isaac King lives too far away. There are plenty of builders around here that are just as good."

Ruth's house had been sold to Peter and Ralene, and Sarah had been home for weeks.

"How would you know anything about building?"

"I mean, I'm sure there are good builders, in fact, excellent builders around these parts. I'll ask Naomi, she knows everyone better than I do."

Her mother folded her arms tightly across her

chest. "What's wrong with you?"

"Me?"

Her mother nodded.

"What do you mean?" Sarah asked.

"Did you have a falling out with the man?"

"Isaac?"

Her mother stared at her with beady eyes and nodded.

"*Nee,* of course, not. I never have arguments with people."

"*Gut!* Then you'll get him on the phone and ask him to come and do the work."

Sarah groaned. She knew Isaac would come there, but did she really want him there? It would be awkward to have someone in the house under her feet in the last couple of months of her pregnancy. And if Isaac didn't stay with them, where would he stay? "How long does it take to build a *grossdaddi haus?*"

"I'm not the one you should be asking that of."

Sarah sighed. "Well, would Isaac stay here, or where would he stay?"

"He can't stay here with you in *your* state. He can stay with that woman next door—the one who's over here all the time since you've been back."

"Her name's Naomi, *Mamm.*"

Her mother's lips turned down.

"Jah, Naomi probably wouldn't mind, and Isaac would be nice and close for managing the building."

"That's settled! Call him!" her mother insisted.

"Mamm, I'll have to ask Naomi and Abe if it's okay if he stays with them first."

"It will be."

"I'm guessing it will be too, but we can't tell them someone's going to be staying with them. We'll have to ask them—it's only polite."

Ruth narrowed her eyes. "You seem fairly certain that Isaac will agree to coming here. Is there something you want to tell me?"

"He's your friend, and he likes you. You were talking like you were certain he'd do it."

Ruth laughed. *"Jah,* I know. Well, what are you standing around here for? Go and ask that woman from next door."

Sarah rolled her eyes and walked out of the house without uttering another word. What was the point of talking when her mother had an answer for everything?

Sarah pushed open Naomi's back door and stuck her head inside. "Hello?"

"Come in," Naomi called.

Sarah walked into the kitchen and saw Naomi at the stove.

"Cooking dinner?"

"*Jah,* just finished—good timing. I'll put the pot on. Your *mudder* has let you out of her sight?"

"Only to ask you a favor."

"What is it?"

"Now that her *haus* has sold, she wants you to have a builder stay with you while he builds the *grossdaddi haus* for her."

"We'd be happy for someone to stay with us. We've got the spare room, as you know. Who is it?"

"Isaac King."

A smirk swept across Naomi's face. *"The* Isaac King?"

"Don't be like that. He's just a friend."

"A friend you haven't stopped talking about in the six weeks you've been back."

Sarah placed her elbow on the table and rested her chin in her cupped palm. "Really? Have I talked about him that much?"

"Jah, you have."

"I didn't realize. *Mamm* wants me to call him and ask him to come here. I know he'll agree to it."

"You told me all about it. He hinted at coming here to build it."

"I told you that?"

"Amongst other things. Isaac this, Isaac that— that's all you've talked about since you've been back—Isaac King."

Sarah laughed. "Now you're exaggerating."

"Maybe a little. I'm not exaggerating when I say your face lights up when you talk about him."

"We had some nice conversations. And we've had similar things happen to us in our lives. It's nice to talk with someone who understands you."

"Use the phone. Call him now. When you come back, you'll be in time for a cup of hot tea."

"Don't you have to ask Abe first?"

"*Nee.* He loves having people come to stay. He's told me it's okay for me to say yes to such a request."

"It might be for many months, or however long it takes to build it."

"I think Abe and I will manage a visitor for that long."

Sarah took a deep breath, nervous about calling him. "I'll have to go back to the *haus* and get his phone number."

"The sooner you go the sooner you get to speak to him."

As Sarah stood, she smiled at her friend, unsure of what she meant. It wasn't as though she had a crush on Isaac King—she was far too old to have a crush, and besides, she was recently widowed with a child on the way. To have feelings for a man at this stage of her life was unseemly. And yet, she couldn't deny the nervousness mixed with excitement that swirled in her stomach at the thought of hearing his voice.

"Isaac?"

"Is that you, Sarah?"

"Jah, it's me."

"It's nice to hear from you."

"Denke." Sarah frowned at her response. Should she thank him after he'd said that? She wasn't certain. The best course of action was to keep talking, she figured. "The reason I'm calling is that my *mudder* is insisting that the only person who can build her *grossdaddi haus* is you."

He gave a low chuckle, and then there was an awkward silence.

"Will… will you?"

"Really? You want me to come there and do the building work?"

"Jah, I do. I mean, my *mudder* does, but I do too, of course."

"It would make me happy to see the both of you again."

"So you'll do it?"

"How soon do you want it built?"

"*Mamm* wants it as soon as possible. I spoke to my neighbor and she and her husband are happy to have you stay with them while you're doing the work."

"Naomi and Abe?"

"*Jah.*" Sarah was surprised that he'd remembered their names.

"I'd be more than happy. You've made my day. Are you calling from Naomi's phone?"

"*Jah,* I am."

Isaac took Naomi's phone number down so he could call back when he'd made travel arrangements.

"*Denke*, I really appreciate this. *Mamm* will be pleased, but she said she must insist on paying you properly for such a big job."

"We'll sort that out when I get there. And how have you been, Sarah."

There it was—the churning in her stomach again as soon as he said her name. "I'm fine, the *boppli* and I are both fine."

"I'm glad to hear all's *gut.* I suppose your *mudder* wants the place built before the *boppli* arrives."

"That's only a few months away. You might not be able to build it in that time."

"I'll get a better idea of a time frame when I come there and see the *haus* and find out exactly how Ruth wants it."

It was ten minutes later that Sarah hung up the phone. She clutched her stomach as she hurried back to Naomi.

"Well, that took a long time." Naomi looked down at the tea she'd poured for Sarah as she stood up. "I'll make you a fresh cup."

"Denke. " Sarah sat down at the table.

"What did he say?"

"He said he'd do it. He's coming here."

"Gut! I can't wait to meet him."

"You'll like him. He's very easy to get along with."

"He must be if he gets along with your *mudder* and she with him."

Sarah giggled. "That's true enough. He's calling back here after he makes the travel arrangements."

"I'll keep a listen out for the phone."

"*Denke. Mamm* will be mighty pleased he's coming here."

"She always seems to get her way. She bullies you, you know."

"She's an old lady. I don't like to disappoint her."

"That'll never happen. You're far too nice and too patient. I don't know how you hold your tongue with her sometimes."

"She's my *mudder*—I have to. I'm kind of glad she wanted the *grossdaddi haus* built on. I was hesitant at first, but now I know it will work out better for everyone, and especially now with the *boppli* coming."

Chapter 15

I have not hid thy righteousness within my heart;
I have declared thy faithfulness and thy salvation:
I have not concealed thy lovingkindness
and thy truth from the great congregation.
Psalm 40:10

Isaac pulled up to Sarah's house in a taxi. He had insisted on catching one from the bus station, although Sarah had wanted to meet him there herself. Before Sarah took him to Naomi's house she planned for them to have an early dinner at her place.

When Ruth and Sarah heard the taxi, they opened the front door. Ruth rushed out to meet Isaac as he stepped out of the taxi.

Sarah stood still, not knowing what to do. Should she go out to greet him with her mother, or did that seem too eager? She stood by the door feeling awkward. Once Isaac retrieved his luggage from the trunk, he looked up, noticed her in the doorway and gave her a wave.

She smiled and waved back. When the taxi drove off, Isaac stood for a few minutes talking with her mother before they made their way to the house.

Were they talking about her, Sarah wondered. They couldn't have been talking about the house because they weren't even looking at the house at the time.

"It's nice to see you again, Sarah," he said when he stepped up on the porch.

"It's nice to see you too, Isaac."

"Just leave your bag at the door, and Sarah will take you to the woman next door's *haus* after dinner," Ruth instructed.

Isaac obeyed and placed his suitcase by the door as Ruth had suggested.

Sarah said, "It's Naomi, *Mamm;* her name's Naomi. Do you keep forgetting?"

Her mother stared at her and blinked a couple of times. *"Jah,* I do keep forgetting; it's a hard name to remember."

As they walked into the house, Sarah whispered

to her mother, "Please try to remember her name. It's not that difficult. She's been my best friend for years, I've written about her in my letters and you've been living right by her for weeks now."

"Only weeks? It feels like months."

Sarah sighed. "Well for most of that time I was staying at your place, so I don't know what you're complaining about."

Her mother wasn't listening and was directing Isaac to the couch. "You must be so tired."

"Nee, I had a few hours sleep on the bus."

"That's good, isn't it, Sarah?" Her mother looked around for her. "Sit down with us, Sarah."

"I was just about to ask Isaac if he'd like some tea or *kaffe."*

"Nee, I'm good, *denke,"* Isaac answered.

Her mother frowned at Sarah and patted the couch next to her. Sarah took the hint and sat by her.

"You'll have to tell me how big you want your *grossdaddi haus,* Ruth." Isaac looked at Sarah. "Or are you the one making the decisions about it,

Sarah?"

Sarah glanced at her mother. "It's my *mudder's* decision. She always gets her own way no matter what I say."

Ruth laughed. "We won't bother you with all that today, Isaac. There's plenty of time to do that tomorrow. There's no rush. That woman next door said you could stay as long as you like."

When Sarah gave her mother a glare, her mother added, "I mean Naomi. Happy now, Sarah?"

Sarah nodded. *"Jah."*

"I suppose you two got to know each other quite well?" She stared at Isaac and then looked at Sarah.

Isaac was the first to respond. *"Jah,* we had some long conversations. I was at your *haus* nearly every day, Ruth. It seems a large place you've got here, Sarah. Wouldn't there be room enough for the two of you here."

"Nee!" Ruth and Sarah chorused at the same time.

"My *mudder* and I are intent on having our own space."

"I don't want to be woken up by crying or screaming—not at my age."

"Perhaps if you'd written to me and asked some questions before you arrived I could've told you what was happening."

"What? Meaning your situation?"

"It's called a pregnancy, *Mamm.*"

"I don't know why you couldn't have told me. I am your *mudder* after all."

"Thomas and I wanted to keep it quiet for a while."

Ruth folded her arms across her chest. "That just doesn't make sense."

"It did to us at the time." Sarah glanced at Isaac and saw him looking uncomfortable with her and her mother niggling at one another. It was probably clear to him by now why living under the one roof wouldn't work for either of them.

"What do you think about the whole thing, Isaac?" Ruth asked.

He laughed. "Don't bring me into this. I will say that if Sarah and Thomas wanted to keep things quiet for a while then that was their decision to make. Is that what you were asking, Ruth?"

Ruth's mouth turned down at the corners.

"Why don't we all go through to the kitchen? Dinner isn't quite ready yet, but I can make you some *kaffe*. How does that sound?"

Isaac's green eyes twinkled. "That sounds perfect."

Even though Isaac had just passed up an offer of coffee, he gave Sarah a big smile and she knew he was grateful to get away from an awkward conversation.

Ruth and Isaac followed Sarah into the kitchen.

"You two sit, and I'll make the *kaffe*," Ruth said. "I can't do everything at my age, but I can still make myself useful."

"We've got that apple and date cake too, *Mamm*."

"I know, I know. You entertain our guest while I fix some things."

Sarah felt Isaac staring at her as they sat down at the table.

"How have you been, Sarah?"

140

"I'm very well; and you?"

He nodded. "I'm fine too."

"And are the young couple settling well into my *mudder's* old *haus?"*

"Jah, they're very pleased with it."

It was awkward for Sarah talking with Isaac and having her mother listening. She realized now how close she and Isaac had become during her stay at her mother's house. When she saw Isaac looking at the table, she knew that Isaac felt just as uncomfortable as she.

Chapter 16

For the which cause I also suffer these things:
nevertheless I am not ashamed:
for I know whom I have believed,
and am persuaded that he is able to keep that
which I have committed unto him against that day.
2 Timothy 1:12

"**W**hat do you think of Isaac?" Naomi asked Sarah a week later as they sat at Naomi's kitchen table.

"You know exactly what I think of him."

Naomi stared at her.

"Don't look at me like that. We have a special connection as friends, but that's all it can be."

"Any other time I'd agree with you, but don't forget about your *boppli.*"

"I can hardly forget—look at me." Sarah leaned back in her chair and placed her hand over her stomach.

Naomi put her fingertips to her mouth and

laughed. "I didn't mean that."

"I know you think my *boppli* needs a *vadder*. Things didn't work out that way. I'm not going to marry solely for that reason—not at my age. *Gott* granted me one last blessing and I don't think He made a mistake. He took Thomas away knowing I was pregnant and that's how He planned it."

"Maybe." Naomi leaned in and whispered, "I heard Abe and Isaac talking and…"

"Naomi, you shouldn't listen in."

"I did. Do you want to know what I heard or not?"

"Okay. As long as it's not something bad."

"Isaac said he liked it here."

Sarah stared at her friend. "Is that it? That's the big thing you overheard?"

"And—I'm not finished—and he said he's pleased to be away from the community back home for a time."

"*Jah*, he's pleased because there are a few women there who think that he should marry them."

Naomi's eyes grew wide. "You didn't tell me

that. Who were they? I know some people there."

"Don't! I'm not going to start spreading rumors."

"They aren't rumors if they're true."

"I don't even know if I remember their names. And don't you breathe a word of this to anyone, but as I said, I think that's why he's pleased to be away. When I first arrived at his *haus,* he thought I was another single lady giving him a pie."

Naomi laughed. "That's hardly a *gut* start."

"We became friends. I feel happy when I'm around him."

"He thinks highly of Ruth from what I've heard."

"I know, and you should see them together. My *mudder* is pleasant to him."

Naomi shook her head. "It's incredible."

"I know. They've always gotten along well; that's why he was pleased to come and build the *grossdaddi haus* for her."

"Maybe that's not the only reason he came here."

"Why? Did he say anything?"

"He doesn't need to. I can tell whenever you're around that he likes you."

145

"I like him too, but I know enough about him to know that he doesn't want any involvement that might lead to marriage."

"You discussed it?"

"Jah, but not directly. I know we both feel the same. We talked about things. He talked about his late wife, Veronica, and I talked about Thomas."

"You must have a strong connection. You don't talk to many people."

"I talk to everyone."

"Sometimes."

Sarah knew that Naomi was trying to push her toward Isaac. That would be the last thing that Isaac wanted. "Naomi, I know you mean well, but nothing's going to happen between Isaac and me. Nothing at all."

A smile flickered across Naomi's face. "Okay."

"I mean it. If I did want something to happen, there'd be nothing I could do about it because that would only scare him away."

"It would only scare him if he knew you liked him or if you did something about it. The best advice I can give you is to appear as though you're not interested. If I know anything about men, that'll have him wondering about you."

"You're dreadful."

"I can picture the two of you together."

"I'm sure you can. I've had too much happening to even consider Isaac as a husband."

The front door sounded and both women looked at each other. Naomi jumped up and looked out the kitchen window.

"What is it?" Sarah whispered.

"That was Isaac. He just walked out of the *haus.* Do you think he heard us talking about him?"

Sarah's face flushed with heat, and she pushed herself out of the chair to join Naomi at the window. "I hope he didn't hear us." Sarah watched him walking to the barn.

"He might have. I thought he was next door with Ruth."

Sarah said, *"Nee,* he wasn't. I thought he must've been somewhere with Abe when I came in and you were here alone."

"He must've been in his room."

The women looked at each other.

"We didn't say anything bad, did we?" Naomi asked.

"Nee, but now he knows I like him." He also would've heard her say that things were too hectic for her to consider a relationship with him. Perhaps that was a good thing. It was best for Isaac and her to each know exactly how the other felt.

"Hasn't he started building yet?" Naomi asked.

"Nee, he's waiting on some tools and materials to be delivered tomorrow."

"I thought he'd begun today. I feel dreadful."

"It doesn't matter. He's not one to be upset by things," Sarah said.

"I suppose not. If you're sure that everything you said was true."

"I'm a practical person. Everything I said was feasible."

When Sarah walked back home, she wondered if Isaac would consider another marriage. Was it just that he didn't find any of the pie ladies suitable?

Did he find her suitable? She felt in her heart that he might. He'd told her back in Ohio that he liked her.

"Sarah."

She swung around to see Isaac standing just outside of her neighbor's barn. "There you are."

"Were you looking for me?" he asked walking toward her.

"Nee." Now she felt silly.

He laughed and she wondered if she'd have to confess her conversation with her friend if he'd overheard it. She inhaled deeply and waited for him to mention something.

"I just wanted to go over the plans with you. I've got them in the barn if you want to come and take a look."

"I'll be happy to, but anything my *mudder* wants will be okay with me."

"It's going onto your *haus,* so I think you should take a look."

Sarah nodded and together they headed to Naomi's barn.

"How are you settling in with Naomi and Abe?"

"Very well. I felt like I knew them as soon as I met them."

"They're lovely people."

"They are."

He spread the plans out and described the dimensions and showed her how it would be joined to her house.

"That suits the place and it will blend in well. I'm so glad *Mamm* insisted on you coming here."

"You're not agreeing with Ruth, are you?"

Sarah looked across at him, amazed. "I guess I am. She might be right about some things."

They both laughed.

"I'm glad I came here." He stared at her and she had to look away.

"*Denke* for showing me the plans. That'll suit *Mamm* just fine."

He nodded as he folded the large paper. "I hope so."

"If you'll excuse me, I've got something urgent I have to tend to back at the *haus.*"

Sarah hurried out of the barn without another word.

Isaac watched Sarah hurrying away from him and wished she were hurrying to him. If she hadn't been so recently widowed he would've laid his heart on the line and told her exactly how he felt about her. It was only that he didn't want to pressure her, and that was the only reason he kept quiet. From his own experience with the 'pie ladies,' he knew what unwanted attention felt like and he couldn't inflict that upon the woman he was growing extremely fond of.

He had already known he liked Sarah back in Ohio, but when he saw her again standing on the porch of her home, his heart told him that here was a woman he would like to marry. A second marriage was something he had thought he'd never consider, but that was before Sarah had come into his life.

Chapter 17

My tongue also shall talk of thy righteousness
all the day long: for they are confounded,
for they are brought unto shame, that seek my hurt.
Psalm 71:24

Sarah hurried into the house and slammed the kitchen door shut behind her. She was fairly certain that Isaac liked her, and she liked him too, but she just couldn't cope with anything else right now. Thomas had passed away only months before and soon she was having a baby. Another man was the last thing she needed. Why hadn't he come along in three or four years? The timing was off.

"What did you slam the door for?" Her mother walked into the kitchen.

"No reason."

"Well don't do it again. I've got sensitive ears."

"Since when?"

"Since... since forever, I suppose. That's why I don't want to be around a crying child. I've told you all this before."

"I'm sorry. I didn't realize it was because of your sensitive ears."

"I thought I mentioned it."

Sarah shook her head. *"Nee,* you didn't." She didn't want her mother to feel uncomfortable or unwelcome, so she added, "Never mind. Now, what would you like for dinner tonight?"

"I've asked Isaac to come for dinner."

"Tonight?"

"Jah, tonight."

"I would've gone to the store again if I'd known."

"Why? To impress him?"

"Nee, Mamm. He's been *gut* to both of us. I'd like to cook him a nice meal."

Her mother chortled. "He's coming to show us both the design he's drawn up."

Sarah kept quiet about seeing it moments before. "That'll be *gut,* then."

"Jah. He's got a pretty good idea of how I want things to be."

When Isaac arrived for dinner, he had a quiet word with Sarah while her mother was in the kitchen.

"I'm afraid I've got some bad news."

"What?"

He laughed. "It's not bad news for you. It's most likely good for you, but bad for me."

"Tell me."

"Abe has got some men to help me with the building work so it'll be done before your baby is born."

"That's kind of him. Why's that bad for you."

"That means I won't have an excuse to be around here as long as I hoped."

"You can stay as long as you like, Isaac. You're a friend to both my mother and me."

He laughed and then took a deep breath. "I can't stay forever. I'll have to go sooner or later. The last thing you need is me hanging around getting in your way."

She looked at him and knew he was fishing for her to say something to the effect that she wanted him around. "You're not in my way."

"I just thought I'd put you in the picture of what's going to be happening."

"Denke."

"Here you are, Isaac. Ready to sample my *dochder's* cooking?"

Sarah sighed.

* * *

With the extra men helping it only took four weeks to complete the *grossdaddi haus* from start to finish. Two days later, Isaac was gone.

Sarah walked into the *grossdaddi haus* to tell her mother something, and burst out crying.

"Whatever is the matter with you?" her mother asked.

"I'm just feeling extra emotional."

"Jah, I remember experiencing that too, when I was in your state."

Sarah knew that wasn't the reason, but she wasn't about to tell her mother that she was crying because she missed her friend.

She wiped her face with the back of a hand. "The place looks lovely, *Mamm.* You were right to have Isaac come here and build it for you."

"I'm right about a lot of things. I'm glad you've come to realize that."

Sarah gave a little laugh. It was nice to have her mother there for company after all. They didn't get along most of the time, but they were family and it was comforting to have her mother close by.

"What do you think of Isaac?"

She stared at her mother. "In what way do you mean exactly?"

"Would you ever consider him as a husband?"

"It's too early to say anything like that, *Mamm.*"

"You're not getting any younger. I've tried to help him find a *fraa.* I told a few ladies in the community that he liked them. I encouraged them to make him pies."

"You're responsible for the pies? The pie ladies was all your doing?"

"Pie ladies? Whatever do you mean?"

"The first time I went to his *haus,* he had a row of pies on his kitchen counter."

"You see? Some people listen to your *mudder,* just not her *kinner* it seems."

Sarah giggled.

"Now that I've got the house finished you can have your boppli."

Sarah pushed out her stomach. "Say that a little louder and one of your relations might listen to you."

"I never went over my expected date."

"Did they have expected dates back then?"

"Don't be sassy."

"A few days over the expected date is normal, I'm told. Even two or three weeks late, but I hope that won't happen to me." Sarah pulled a face. She was ready for her baby to come out now. Any longer and she felt she would burst.

"We can't order the child to arrive on this day or that day."

"Jah, I know you're not ordering the *boppli* to come, *Mudder."*

Her mother pulled a face. "I'll pray that you don't have to wait too long."

Sarah only had to wait another three days for her baby to arrive.

Chapter 18

Let no man despise thy youth;
but be thou an example of the believers,
in word, in conversation, in charity,
in spirit, in faith, in purity.
1 Timothy 4:12

Three weeks later

"I hope David didn't keep you up all night, *Mamm.*" Sarah had named her baby boy David. She was nearly going to name him Thomas after his father, but knew her mother would end up calling him Tom. It would remind her how Thomas and her mother never got along. She wanted a new beginning in her relationship with her mother—a new beginning where they compromised on things.

"I didn't hear a thing."

"Really? You heard nothing?"

"Nee."

"That's good."

Sarah considered it a waste of money that her mother had had the *grossdaddi haus* added on to her own home. Ruth was constantly at Sarah's house for meals. Ruth slept at her place and that was all.

"I do have some concerns."

"I'm sorry but we can't send him back now, it's too late." Sarah giggled.

"What?"

"Don't worry, *Mudder*. I was just making a joke about sending David back."

Her mother stared at her and then said, "I was talking about the concerns I have with the quality of the building work at my little *haus.*"

"What's wrong with it?"

"I have concerns that there are a few things that are not quite right."

"What kind of things?"

"Things like the windows are sticking and the doors aren't shutting properly."

"I'll talk to Abe. I'm sure it's under some sort of warranty or something. I'll see if he can speak with the men who helped Isaac."

"Nee, that wouldn't be right. I'm not having anybody look at the property except for Isaac."

"He lives too far away, *Mamm*, we can't bother him with things like that."

"He did the work, so he's responsible. He would be only too happy to come back and fix a few things. Don't you want him back here?"

"I do, but I can't be selfish. The two of us became good friends."

"Yes, I know that. And that's exactly why he would like to come out and fix those few things."

"Jah, but are there enough things for him to come back? I don't want him to come back all this way for nothing."

"I paid a lot of money to get this place added on to your *haus*. I would think you'd want me to be comfortable and fully secure in the place."

"Okay, *Mamm,* do it if you wish. If you want him to come out and check over the place, you could write to him and see what he says."

"I don't need to write to him if you can just ring

him up from your friend's place."

"And what friend would that be?"

"Naomi. I know her name. Anyway, as I was saying, you can ring him and see when he can come back."

Sarah nodded, but had a different idea. She would ask him who he would recommend for them to have take a look over the place. Surely one of the men who'd helped him build the place wouldn't mind coming back, especially when Sarah was certain that it was all in her mother's imagination.

"Can you do me up a list of what's wrong with the place before I call him?"

"He'll see when he gets here."

"That's not how things work, *Mamm*. You need to tell him so he can see if it's worth him coming all this way. Otherwise, Abe can recommend someone local to us."

"I told you, I only want Isaac to come here. I know you're getting older, but I didn't know you were losing your hearing."

"Okay, *Mamm,* I will do it but only if you write

me a list. If you don't give me a list, I'll speak to Abe about it."

Her mother sighed. "You're so stubborn sometimes."

"It's called compromising, *Mamm.*" She paused. "And maybe genetics."

* * *

"Hello, Isaac."

"Is that you, Sarah?"

Sarah's heart pounded at hearing his voice. *"Jah,* it is." They'd been writing but this was the first time they'd spoken on the phone since he'd gone back to Ohio.

"Is everything all right? David's okay, isn't he?"

"He's fine and I'm sorry to bother you, but my *mudder* is insisting there are things wrong with the *grossdaddi haus* that you'll need to fix."

"What are they?"

Sarah read from the list her mother had given her. When she finished, there was silence on the other end of the line. "I'm sorry to bother you with this. She's just being picky. I wanted Abe to give me the name of one of the men who helped you build it. They live a lot closer than you."

"Does she want me to come back?"

"*Jah,* she does."

"I'm finishing off a job that'll take me through until the end of the week, but I could come after that."

"That'd be *wunderbaar. Mamm* will be so pleased."

"It'll give me a chance to meet David."

"He's a fine *bu.* He's big for his age, and his eyes are the bluest of blue, just like Thomas.'"

"I'll call Abe to see if I can stay with him and Naomi for a couple of days."

"Oh, I didn't even think of that. Do you want me to ask them for you?"

"*Nee.* I know them well enough now. I've got their number somewhere. I'll call them later today."

"*Denke*, Isaac. I really appreciate you going out of your way like this."

"Anything for you and for Ruth."

A giggle escaped her lips.

"How have you been? I got your letters, but it's nice to hear your voice."

"I've been fine."

"And have you and Ruth been getting along?"

"We have—well, we get along with each other most of the time. We had a big talk the other day about compromising."

"I'm glad to hear that. Well, I better carry on with what I'm doing. The sooner I finish my work here, the sooner I can get to your place."

"Okay, bye, Isaac."

"Bye, Sarah, and it's really good to hear from you."

Sarah hung up the phone. She'd asked Naomi to borrow their phone, and of course Naomi would be wondering whom Sarah had to call.

"Well?"

She spun around and saw Naomi standing there. *"Ach!* You gave me a fright."

"Was that Isaac?"

"How did you know?"

"Because you were in a daydream. Is David having a nap?"

"Nee, and I've left him with *Mamm."*

Naomi pulled a face. "That's not good. Go and get him and bring him back here. I'll make us a cup of hot tea and you can tell me all about it."

Sarah smiled. "There's nothing to tell."

"Hurry, you've left David with your *mudder.* What if he cries?—she hates that."

Sarah started walking. "If he cries, I won't hear the end of it for a week. I'll be right back."

Naomi giggled. "I'll put the pot on the stove."

Sarah peeped through her kitchen window when she arrived back to a silent house. She saw her mother sitting quietly, cradling David in her arms and talking to him. This didn't look like the same woman who'd told her she'd had enough of babies.

She pushed open the kitchen door and walked through.

"Finally. I thought you'd never come back. What

did Isaac say?"

"He said he'd finish off what he's working on and come here."

A huge grin broke out onto her mother's face. "Very good."

"I'm going back to Naomi's *haus* now for a cup of hot tea. Would you like to come?" Sarah already knew the answer. Naomi and her mother still didn't get along.

"Nee, I'll just sit here by myself. An old unwanted lady left alone while her *dochder* goes to tend to others."

Sarah refused to take the bait. "Sounds *gut!*" She reached out and lifted David out of her mother's arms.

"I can watch him."

"You never want to watch him."

"Well, he'll keep me company while you go gallivanting."

"I'm only going to be next door for half an hour."

"And I'm supposed to do what while you're gone?"

"I said you could come with me."

"Naomi wouldn't like me over there."

"You could try to be a little friendlier with her."

"Just leave the little one with me."

"What if he cries?"

"All of them cry. It's just a message to big people that they need something."

Sarah wondered if her mother had suddenly taken ill. "Do you feel all right?"

"I do. Why?"

"You've never wanted anything to do with him—with David."

"He likes me. He smiled at me."

"Okay. We can give this a try. I'll leave him with you for half an hour. He was fed not long ago so he should be all right for a while."

Her mother reached up for David and Sarah placed her baby in her mother's arms. "Are you sure about this?"

"I'm his *grossmammi*. Just go would you? We won't be alone if we're together, will we, David?"

That was the first time she'd witnessed her

mother speaking to him. And she'd even used his name. "I'll go now, then. I won't be long."

Her mother didn't reply, so Sarah hurried over to Naomi's *haus*. As much as she loved David, it was nice to have a small amount of free time.

"Where's David?"

"My *mudder* has him."

"Really?"

"Jah, and what's more she was the one who offered to look after him. Insisted, actually."

"That's the strangest thing I've ever heard. I thought she didn't want anything to do with him. Isn't that why she wanted the *grossdaddi haus* built?"

"Funny you should mention that." Sarah proceeded to tell her friend about her mother's demands and the forthcoming visit of Isaac. "I guess I shouldn't have mentioned anything to you at this stage. Isaac said he'd call you and see if it was all right that he stay with you again."

"Of course it will be. He was great to have around. He was good with the *kinner."*

"I don't know how you do it with six *kinner.* I'm at my wit's end sometimes with only one."

"The first one's always the hardest because you don't know what to expect. By the time the second one comes along, you've got it all worked out."

"There won't be a second one for me."

"I shouldn't have said that. I'm sorry."

"Don't be. It's just the way things are. I'm grateful for the one that I have. Things could've been very different."

"It'll get easier as David grows."

"I hope so."

"It will, I promise. And now it seems you're getting Ruth trained to look after him."

"Jah, that was an unexpected thing."

"Ach, the tea." Naomi stood up to make the tea. As she sat back down and passed a cup of tea to Sarah, she said, "Now tell me how you feel about Isaac coming back."

"I'll be pleased to see him."

Naomi searched her face. "You can't hide anything from me."

"I'm not. I like him and you know that. But, I'm not a young woman anymore. I'm over forty and now I've got my *mudder* living with me."

"That's perfect. He gets on well with Ruth."

"I'm scared."

"Of what?"

"What if he gets sick like Thomas did? I don't know if I can do it all again."

"Gott gives us strength when we need it, not before. Things will work out if you trust that they will. It all depends what you want. Your life will be easier with a man to look after you."

"I can look after myself."

"Jah, but it's not nearly as much fun on your own. You must get lonely."

"I do. I have no man to share David with. It would be nice to have a man who would love him as much as I do and then we could watch him grow together. It won't be too long and he'll be walking."

"Do you love Isaac?"

Sarah took a sip of tea and slowly lowered the cup to the saucer while she thought. "I don't know.

I like having him around."

"That's a start."

"But how do I know I'll be happy if I marry again? I loved Thomas, but then I watched him slip away from me before my very eyes. It was as though he was taken from me little by little for some time before he died."

"You can't compare what you had with Thomas with what you might have with someone else. If you marry again it doesn't mean that you didn't love Thomas and don't still love him."

"I'm glad you said that. I was worried when I first met Isaac and started to like him. Everything within me was in turmoil and confusion that I liked another man. It didn't seem to make any sense. I certainly wasn't looking for a husband. I hadn't even thought about it, not for a split second even."

"Sometimes things work like that. Emma Hesh got married just one year after her first husband died. They met at his funeral."

"Who's Emma Hesh?"

"She's my cousin from Idaho. Now she writes

that she's never been happier."

"How long has she been married now?"

"Around five years."

"I'm glad things worked out for her."

"They will for you too."

"I'm sure they will, but I guess I have to figure out what I want."

"Don't leave things too long. Remember those pie ladies you told me about."

Sarah slowly nodded before she realized her friend was joking, and then she laughed when she saw Naomi's face. Inside, Sarah wasn't laughing. For the first time since she met Isaac, she wondered if one of the pie ladies might wear him down.

How would she feel if he suddenly married one of them?

Chapter 19

I will go in the strength of the Lord God:
I will make mention of thy righteousness,
even of thine only.
Psalm 71:16

Today was the day that Isaac was coming back to look at what was 'wrong' with the *grossdaddi haus*. Sarah knew in her heart that there was nothing wrong with it. What was her mother playing at?

"Here he is," her mother said from the couch in Sarah's living room, where they'd been waiting for Isaac to arrive.

Sarah stood and saw the taxi pulling up at her house.

"Aren't you coming out to greet him, *Mamm?*"

"*Nee.* You go out and see him. I'm a little tired this morning."

Sarah stared hard at her mother. Now she knew for sure and for certain that her mother was trying to match her with Isaac. Had this been her plan all along? Sarah could tell by the smirk on her mother's face as she sat there with her hands clasped firmly in her lap that she was plotting. "I know you're up to something, *Mamm*. And I intend to find out exactly what it is."

"I'm not up to anything. Now you'd better go out and greet our visitor."

Sarah took a deep breath and went to meet Isaac. As soon as she stepped out of the house, she looked up to see Isaac standing there staring at her. She couldn't help but smile.

While the taxi driver retrieved his suitcase from the trunk, he walked toward her.

"You look well, Sarah."

"So do you."

"Where's David?"

"He's upstairs sleeping."

"I'm looking forward to seeing him."

"I hope we haven't called you all this way for nothing." She leaned in and whispered, "I think *Mamm* is being a bit dramatic about the things that she thinks are wrong with the place."

He frowned. "Well I suppose there's only one way to find out."

"Mamm is waiting for you in the living room. Come inside and sit down for a moment."

After Isaac paid the taxi driver, he picked up his suitcase and followed Sarah into the house.

When he and her mother had greeted each other, Sarah asked, "Would you like *kaffe,* Isaac?"

"I'll have tea," her mother said before Isaac had a chance to respond.

"I'd like *kaffe.* I'll come and help you with it," Isaac said.

"Okay. You're not too tired?"

"I'm fine," he said.

She picked up the pot to fill it with water and he took it from her hands.

"I'll do that," he said.

"I'm perfectly capable of doing it."

"Now that I'm here you don't have to do it." He flashed her a big smile.

Right at that moment, she knew that she didn't

want him to leave. She'd been so upset last time he'd left and it would only be harder this time. The only thing was she had to figure out whether she was in love with him or whether it was nothing more than him being a good friend.

"I've been selfish," she said.

"I can't believe that. What have you been selfish about?"

"I've told Naomi and Abe that we are keeping you here for dinner before you go over there tonight."

He laughed. "Thank you. I'm glad. That means I get to spend more time with you and David."

"Do you want to see him now while the water's boiling?"

"I'd love to."

"Follow me."

They climbed the stairs and she pushed the bedroom door open. There he was, sleeping in the cradle on his back with his arms over his head.

"He is so precious and beautiful," Isaac whispered. "How does it feel to be a mother?"

"It's given me a new appreciation for my own mother."

He chuckled. "You are blessed, you know."

"Yes, I know it." She nodded and then she looked at him. "I've made your favorite, lamb stew with vegetables for tonight."

"Denke."

"I don't know if it'll be as *gut* as yours."

"I'm certain it will be."

She smiled and looked back at David.

"How is your mother doing with him?"

"She's doting on him. She's cooing and talking to him. It's not at all what I expected. And she's amazed that he hardly ever cries."

"A contented infant seldom cries."

"I don't know about that. *Mamm* says it's all to do with the personality. Apparently I was a crying *boppli.*"

He looked back at David. "Will he be awake soon?"

"Probably another hour." She beckoned to him to follow she walked to the door. After they were outside the room, she closed the door quietly.

"Have you seen the things that are wrong with Ruth's place?" he whispered to her as they started down the stairs.

She held the railing, stopped and turned slightly. "I think it's all up here." She tapped the side of her head.

He smiled. "We'll find out tomorrow."

"I hope you haven't come all this way for nothing."

"I was praying for an excuse to see you again."

She smiled at him, turned and walked down the remaining stairs.

"You two took a long time," Ruth said when the pair sat back down in the living room.

Sarah jumped up. "The pot on the stove."

"I forgot too."

"You stay, Isaac. I'll make the *kaffe.*" Sarah hurried to the kitchen, hoping her mother would behave herself. Just in case she didn't, Sarah kept an ear out to hear what might be said in her absence.

"She needs a man around, Isaac, and you've

needed a woman for quite some time."

Sarah shook her head. Her mother had started already. At least she was now openly matchmaking rather than doing it in a sneaky way.

Isaac answered, *"Jah,* and *denke* for telling all those women to cook me pies. I don't know if I can ever look at another one."

"Another pie or another woman?"

Isaac laughed. "Another pie. Or another pie lady."

"What do you think of my Sarah?"

Sarah froze in the kitchen, nearly spilling the boiling water she was pouring into the mug. She never thought her mother would come out so brazenly with something like that.

"She's lovely."

"Why don't you marry her?"

He laughed again. "It takes two."

"So you're in love with her and don't know how she feels?"

"It's not as easy as that, Ruth. My home's not here."

"It could be. What's keeping you in Ohio? I left, you can too."

"*Kaffe* time!" Sarah burst back into the room with coffee and cookies. As she set the tray on the low table, she could feel Isaac's eyes on her. She knew he was wondering if she'd heard what her mother and he had been talking about.

While they drank their hot drinks and talked about other things, Sarah wondered if Isaac might ever consider leaving Ohio. When she realized she was hoping something more would come of their friendship, she snapped herself from her daydreams.

"How long do you plan on staying, Isaac?" Sarah asked.

"It depends on how much work needs to be done on Ruth's place."

Of course, silly question.

"I'll look at it tomorrow in the daylight, first thing."

Sarah nodded.

"First thing? I'm getting picked up tomorrow by

Elspeth Muir. She's taking me to a quilting bee."

"I thought you left off quilting, *Mamm*. Don't your fingers still bother you?"

Ruth set her beady eyes onto Sarah. "More goes on at one of those things than quilting."

"Gossiping?" Sarah asked.

Her mother wagged a finger at her. "That's a dreadful thing to say, Sarah. It's a time of gathering together and a time of fellowship."

Sarah laughed. "I was only joking, *Mamm.*"

Isaac sniggered.

"Anyway, I won't be here in the morning, Isaac. Sarah will have to take you through and show you everything on my list."

This was another scheme in her mother's grand plan. She'd had no interest in quilting for years. It made sense she would try to pick Sarah's next husband because Ruth had never liked her late husband, Thomas.

* * *

"So far I don't see anything wrong with anything. Just some windows that are sticking and that's easy to fix."

"I was afraid that would be the case."

"What's going on with her?"

"Isn't that obvious?"

"It's obvious to me, but I didn't know if it would be obvious to you."

Sarah smiled and, not wanting to embarrass herself, she asked, "What do you think it is?"

"I think she's trying to match the two of us together. Every time you walked out of the room last night she told me how much David needs a *vadder.*"

Sarah put her hand to her head. "I'm so sorry."

"There is nothing for you to be sorry about." He laughed. "You didn't do anything, did you?"

She playfully slapped him on his arm. "Of course I didn't. I had no idea what she was doing. I guess that's not entirely true; it crossed my mind once or twice and then I overheard what she said to you yesterday when I was getting the *kaffe.*"

He slumped into Ruth's couch in her living room. "Well, what do you think we should do about it?"

"I don't know if there's anything to do, unless we tell her to mind her own business, and she is not going to take to kindly to that."

"I didn't mean about Ruth. I meant about us."

"What do you mean?"

"What if Ruth's right about us? We might make a good match."

"I thought you weren't interested in getting married."

"I genuinely wasn't until I met you. I thought that was the last thing I would ever consider. The 'pie ladies' didn't have a chance."

Sarah sank heavily into the couch opposite him. She never thought she would consider another marriage either, but Isaac was one man she could see herself married to. Was he proposing to her? He hadn't asked her straight out, so everything was kind of awkward. She cleared her throat and looked around. "So nothing in this place needs fixing?"

"There are a couple of windows sticking, but

that's all."

Sarah shook her head. "I'm continually amazed by my mother. I can't believe she took David with her to the quilting bee. And I'm amazed that she made you come all this way."

"I don't know why you're so surprised about her taking David with her. She is the *grossmammi* after all."

"When she came here, she told me she would not help me with him and wanted to have a separate place so she wouldn't hear him cry." Talking about David kept the conversation from becoming awkward.

"It appears the little man has captured her heart."

Sarah smiled. "It seems to be that way."

"Now what did we decide about getting married?"

She looked at him wondering if he was joking or whether he was serious.

"We haven't decided anything yet." She thought that was the safest thing to say.

He looked down and gave a small chuckle. Sarah considered another change of subject was needed.

"What are you going to say to Ruth about the things on her list?"

"I'll tell her that everything was in her imagination."

"That won't go down well with her."

He laughed. "What do you think I should say, then?"

"Perhaps you should say that you'll need to stay a few weeks to carefully monitor the ongoing situation."

He laughed and set his green eyes on her. "Is that what you want me to do—stay a few extra weeks?"

She nodded. "I'd like that. If you can."

"That's what I will do, then."

They exchanged smiles.

"Let me take you out somewhere for lunch today."

"I can't today. I told my *mudder* I would collect her and David from the quilting bee and then we're off to the markets."

"Tomorrow?"

She nodded. "I'd like that."

Chapter 20

As the cold of snow in the time of harvest,
so is a faithful messenger to them that send him:
for he refresheth the soul of his masters.
Proverbs 25:13

The next day she told her mother she was going out with Isaac. Her mother offered to look after David for her.

While David was having his morning nap, Ruth sat at the kitchen table watching her daughter wash up from breakfast.

"This might be your last chance, you know."

"My last chance for what?"

"Your last chance for marriage."

"I'm not looking for marriage, *Mamm.*"

"Well you should be. You shouldn't let a good man like Isaac go."

Sarah did her best to ignore her mother while continuing to wash the dishes. "I can't just marry someone because you think they're good, *Mamm.*

It has to be up to me. I know you didn't like Thomas."

"I don't see why my input doesn't matter," her mother muttered. "I'd have to see him a lot too."

Sarah sighed.

"Do you know how many women were chasing him and probably still are?" Ruth asked.

It disturbed Sarah to hear that. She didn't want any other women to be interested in him.

"That bothers you to hear, doesn't it?"

She really wanted to tell her mother to mind her own business, but didn't want her mother to feel unwelcome in her house.

"I know you mean well, but I'm old enough now that you should let me live my life the way I want to live it."

"That's exactly my point; you're middle-aged and not getting any younger. It's very hard for a woman like you to find a husband."

Sarah finished washing the last dish. She knew what her mother said was true. It was easy for the young women to find husbands but not the older widows. Most of them never married again simply because most of the men their age in the community were already married and the older single men often look for younger wives so that they can have a family. It bothered her when her mother was right.

* * *

Isaac was nervous about their first date. He'd tried to propose to Sarah but she had seen it as a joke. He would have to ask her directly if she'd be his wife. That was the only way that she'd know he was serious and not kidding around. His fingers were all over the place as he tried to button his white shirt.

He had told Ruth the day before that his home was back in Ohio, but the truth was he could make his home anywhere. It was the people who surrounded him that formed his home, not a piece of land or a house. He knew when he'd left Lancaster County after building Ruth's *grossdaddi haus* that he wanted to make Sarah his wife. He knew then that it was a matter of patience, waiting for her and hoping one day she'd be ready.

They had exchanged letters and he thought it might take a couple more years of letters going back and forth before he made his next visit to Lancaster County. He was glad it came sooner than that, thanks to Ruth's creativity. He walked downstairs and told Naomi he wouldn't be there for the midday meal.

"I know. Sarah told me."

When he saw the small knowing smile on Naomi face, he inquired further, "And exactly what did Sarah tell you?"

She looked up from kneading the bread. "She told me that the two of you were having lunch together, that's all. Why, is there more?"

He smiled and shook his head. "Not at this stage."

"Ah, but there is the possibility of something more?"

He shook his head again. "You're as bad as

Ruth."

She gasped in an exaggerated manner. "I never thought I would be compared with Ruth."

He smiled and walked through the kitchen towards the back door. "I'll see you later today. Do you want me to pick anything up for you while I'm out?"

"*Nee denke*. I'm okay."

Isaac headed to Sarah's house. It amazed him how many people didn't get along with Ruth, when he had found her a wonderful friend. She'd been good to him over the years. He'd found out from Sarah that Ruth and Sarah's late husband had never gotten along, and it was clear that Naomi didn't get along with Ruth either. There had been off and on tension between Ruth and Sarah, but this time 'round he'd noticed that they were getting along a lot better.

The closer he walked to Sarah's house, the more he knew he didn't want to go home without asking Sarah to marry him. He was hopeful that she would say yes, but he couldn't go back to Ohio without directly asking her. Even if she said 'no,' she would know he was interested.

He didn't like to compare Sarah to his late wife. They had very different personalities, with Veronica being more loud and outgoing than Sarah, who was quiet and seemed happy with her own company. The one thing they had in common was a true and gracious heart, and caring for others.

As soon as he stepped on the porch, Sarah open the door. He looked into her blue eyes and wanted to take her into his arms, hold her, protect her and love her.

He wondered what was in her heart. He'd made it clear that he was fond of her and she had agreed to the lunch together. Perhaps there was a chance for him. Today had to be the day he would ask her to marry. He could wait no longer to ask the question.

"You're right on time," she said with a pretty smile.

"Good. Shall I hitch the buggy or would you prefer to go by taxi?"

"I think it would be nice to go by buggy."

"You stay right there and I'll go and get it ready. Is David coming with us?"

She shook her head. "*Mamm* insisted on looking after him."

Ten minutes later, they were seated in the buggy and ready to go.

"You can direct me to a nice place for lunch, can't you?"

She nodded. "I know just the place."

Isaac clicked the horse forward. In his nervousness, he struggled to find something to talk about. All he wanted was to tell her how he felt about her and how he was pleased to be there. He was glad when she started talking.

"What did my *mudder* say last night when you told her you didn't think there was anything wrong except for the window?"

"I told her what we discussed. I told her I'd have to stick around for a few weeks to monitor the situation."

Sarah laughed. "And what did she say about

that?"

He scratched his eyebrow. "She thought it was a good idea."

Sarah laughed again. "Of course she would've."

As the buggy wound around the narrow roads, he looked up at the clear blue sky. "Looks like we're having a lovely day again today."

"*Jah,* the weather has been unusually warm for this time of year."

There was silence between them for some moments before Sarah had to direct him where to turn. It wasn't an awkward silence, it was a pleasurable quietness—just being in each other's company was a nice feeling.

When they pulled up not far from the restaurant, Isaac said, "Ah, I've noticed this spot before; is this your favourite lunch place?"

"I've never actually been inside. But I've driven past it and I've heard nice things about it. I haven't really had a chance to go out much, with David and *Mamm,* and everything."

He helped her down from the buggy.

"That's understandable. I'm sure they both keep you busy," he said.

"They do."

Together they walked to the restaurant. Once they were inside, a waiter seated them at a table near the window.

Isaac tried to look at the menu, but nerves had taken a hold of him. He didn't feel like eating anything and was tempted just to ask her right then and there and get it off his chest. Then he decided to wait for the right time, rather than have things become awkward and put her on the spot. He wondered what questions he might ask her to see if she would be receptive to marriage, before he made a fool of himself or was rejected.

"What do you feel like eating?" he asked when he looked up from the menu he hadn't really seen.

"I think the mushroom steak looks good."

"Yes, that's what I was thinking. I'll have the same. I haven't had steak in a while." He closed the menu and she closed hers.

It wasn't long before a waiter was upon them to

take their orders.

When the waiter left, Sarah stared at Isaac. "Are you alright today?"

"*Jah*, why?"

"You seem a little distant or something. I can't quite put my finger on it. Have I done something to upset you?"

"*Nee*, you haven't. I don't think you could ever do anything to upset anybody."

She laughed. "I wish that were true. I upset my *mudder* all the time. And I'm sure I probably upset other people too."

He shook his head. "I can't imagine it."

"Well it's true."

"Marry me, Sarah," he blurted out.

"What?"

He stared at her stunned face. He leaned in and said quietly, "Would you, Sarah Hersler, marry me? Or, at least think about it?"

She sucked in her lips and her eyes dropped to the table. At that moment he regretted his hastiness. He should've waited for a better moment.

"I'm sorry. It was selfish of me to ask. I know it's probably too soon for you to consider anything like that. And I don't even know if that's something you'd ever want."

The waiter brought a pitcher of water and a basket of bread to the table. They both stared at the bread in silence.

Chapter 21

Know therefore that the Lord thy God, he is God, the faithful God, which keepeth covenant and mercy with them that love him and keep his commandments to a thousand generations;
Deuteronomy 7:9

Sarah couldn't take her eyes from the bread. She hadn't expected him to propose so suddenly. Not now, not like this. This *was* what she wanted. But how did she know that everything would turn out well for them? She liked him well enough, and if she would let herself admit it, she knew she already loved him.

"I'm uncertain. I guess I'm scared of life and how it can change so suddenly. Thomas and I were happy and then he suddenly got ill and then my life changed. Instead of us having a relationship of husband-and-wife I became his nurse, his caretaker. I had lost the man I married long before he died. And then he did die, and then I became a

203

mudder—with no husband."

She shook her head and stared at the bread once more. "Nothing was as I thought it would be. When I married Thomas, I expected that we would be together forever and raise many *kinner*. Somehow deep in my heart, I feel maybe a little bit cheated. That's the best way I can describe it."

"I know exactly what you mean. It was the same when I married Veronica. We both thought we would grow old together and raise many *kinner*, just like everyone around us. Then when we finally found out we were going to be parents we were thrilled. And then to lose her like I did, and to lose my baby boy, was beyond belief. If I had the choice, I would have asked *Gott* to take me. We can't know the mind of *Gott*. We've both learned that the future has no guarantees."

She nodded and looked into his green eyes. He was right. Tomorrow is never guaranteed; today was all they had. And she wanted to spend all her todays with him if she was honest with herself. Fear was never far from her heart. Just when she tried to be brave, fear came creeping back. She looked into his face; he was waiting for an answer.

"I'm confused about how I feel. Part of me wants to marry you, but the other part of me is scared."

His concerned face broke into a grin. "How about you think on it for awhile? You don't have to decide today, or this week or next month. Take your time."

"Is that alright?"

"Of course that's alright." He chuckled. "I feel much better now that I've asked you. I've been a bundle of nerves trying to figure out how to ask you and when was the right time."

"I feel better too. Now I know how you feel, and I don't have to wonder."

The waiter brought their food to the table.

While they ate, they talked about everything else but marriage. Sarah knew by the end of their lunch date that she wanted him in her life on a permanent basis. She was ready to accept his proposal of marriage. They'd both had bad things happen to them in the past, but what if things were different for both of them this time?

"What are you thinking about, Sarah?"

She looked into his kind green eyes. "I'm thinking about you. I'm thinking that I don't want you to leave and if you have to, I want you to come back real quick."

The lines in his forehead deepened just slightly. "What are you saying?"

"I'm saying that I will marry you."

He smiled, leaned forward and took her hand. "You will?"

"I will."

"What changed your mind?"

"Nothing. I've liked you from the beginning, but it was too soon and then I was scared. I'm still scared. You're right about us only having today. I want all my days to be with you. I feel good when you're around—safe and protected."

"I can work anywhere. Would you feel better if I moved here?"

"Would you really do that?"

"I'd do anything I could to keep you happy."

She felt tears stinging behind her eyes. "I'd like that—if you move here. My *haus* is plenty big enough. I can't promise you any *kinner*, that is, except David. At my age, I don't think I'd be able to have any more."

"David is a blessing—an added blessing for me. I'd gotten used to the idea of not having any *kinner*. I'm not wanting more. If *Gott* chooses us to have another one, so be it." He squeezed her hand slightly. "All I want is you."

She looked down at their hands clasped together on the table not even worried about what other people might think about their display of affection. "Shall we go home and tell *Mamm* the *gut* news?"

He laughed.

"Do you think she'll be shocked?" she asked.

"She'll be pleased that her little scheme worked."

"The scheme of finding things wrong so you'd have to come back here?"

"She'll be pleased all right," he said. "I hope so anyway."

* * *

"Well, it's high time this has happened. I must say I'm shocked."

"Are you really so shocked, *Mamm?*"

"*Jah,* I am. You did inherit my stubborn streak, after all."

She looked her daughter up and down. "You'll be looked after when I'm gone."

Sarah smiled at Isaac and he smiled back at her.

"I'll always look after Sarah, and David too."

"David's asleep. He fell asleep not ten minutes after you left and he's been asleep ever since. Now, when are you two getting married? I wouldn't leave it too long."

Isaac laughed. "I'll have to sort out some things back home. We want to get married as soon as we can."

"I'll be your *mudder*-in-law, Isaac."

"*Jah,* you will."

"Why don't you go home as quick as you can, get things in order and come back and marry my *dochder?*"

"That's kind of what the plan is."

"Gut! Then when you get back you can have a look at one of my doors. It's sticking you know. Just like the windows."

Isaac and Sarah looked at one another. They'd been convinced she had only complained about her place to get him back to Lancaster County. Perhaps they'd been wrong?

* * *

Four weeks later, Sarah and Isaac stood in front of the bishop from Sarah's community in Lancaster County. They looked into each other's eyes as the bishop pronounced them married.

It was a strange feeling for Sarah, as she'd never envisioned or wanted a second marriage. She knew that Isaac felt the same. *Gott* had blessed them both with a second chance at love and had blessed both of them with David.

They held hands as they walked out of Sarah's house where the wedding had taken place.

"Denke, Sarah. You've made me a happy man."

"We've both been blessed to have such happiness at our age."

"I do feel young again."

Sarah giggled. "Me too."

Sarah turned around and looked back at the house to see her mother standing on the porch, with David firmly in her arms, staring after them as they walked to the head table of the wedding feast in the yard. Months before, she'd been distraught when her mother had announced she'd come to stay, but things had quickly changed. Now she couldn't imagine her life without her mother close by.

Isaac, seeing Sarah looking at something, also looked over his shoulder. "I'm glad you two have worked things out."

"It's an ongoing process. Anyway, she's delighted that we're married. She said she was looking forward to having her three favorite people under one roof."

"Really?"

Sarah nodded.

"Just don't tell your siblings about that."

"They wouldn't believe me if I did." Sarah turned back and gave her mother a little wave before she sat down at the wedding table next to Isaac. She closed her eyes and thanked God for her unexpected happiness. And the future—she put her future in His hands not knowing what it might bring, but knowing whatever came her way, *Gott* would always be there right by her side.

Truly my soul waiteth upon God:
from him cometh my salvation.
He only is my rock and my salvation; he is my
defence;
I shall not be greatly moved.
Psalm 62:1

Thank you for your interest in
The Middle-Aged Amish Widow

To join Samantha Price's
email list and be kept up to date with
New Releases subscribe at her website:
http://www.samanthapriceauthor.com

Other books in this series:
Book 1
Amish Widow's Hope

Newly widowed Amish woman, Anita Graber, has returned to live with her brother and his family in Lancaster County. As an expectant widow, she is quite surprised when everyone from the bishop's wife to her brother decides that her baby needs a father. Anita endures many embarrassing moments as she's forced into one awkward situation after another. Even though another man is the last thing on her mind, she finds a friend in her sister-in-law's brother, Simon. Anita wonders why everyone has rejected Simon as a suitable match for her. Will Anita finally convince everyone that she and her baby are happy on their own? Could the man that no one sees her with, be the very man who eventually captures her heart?

Book 2 *Expectant Amish Widows*
The Pregnant Amish Widow

After her husband's death, Grace Stevens returns to her family and her Amish community. She'd suffered through an abusive marriage and wanted nothing more than to get baptized into the Amish faith and begin a new life.

Grace finds it impossible to put the past behind her when Marlene, the woman who caused her to leave the community, was now living in Grace's family home and married to Grace's brother.

More friction occurs between the women when Grace discovers that she's five months pregnant. As Marlene is childless after four years of marriage, she spirals further into depression.

When Grace learns that the man she nearly married is still single, she wonders if they might rekindle what they once had, but her hopes fade when she learns she's not the only woman interested in him.

Can Grace come to terms with having her late husband's baby, forgive Marlene enough to comfort her, and secure the love of the man she once loved so dearly?

Book 3 *Expectant Amish Widows*
Amish Widow's Faith

With her baby only weeks away from being born, Deborah is skilfully avoiding her sister Emily's attempts to match her with someone totally unsuitable. When Emily realizes that Deborah is not interested in the man she chose for her, Emily finds a replacement and throws herself into ensuring that a wedding will take place.

Will Emily be so busy matching others that she cannot see that her own perfect match is right under her nose? Will a visit from a stranger cause Deborah to see that it might be possible to love twice in one lifetime?

Book 4 *Expectant Amish Widows*

Their Son's Amish Baby

As Mr. and Mrs. Stauffer mourn the death of their son, Simon, who died during his *rumspringa,* Bree Fortsworth knocks on their door and announces she is having Simon's baby.

Bree explains she has nowhere else to go and asks if she can stay with them. After they agree to her request she has another and the Stauffers are surprised when Bree wants them to adopt the baby.

After Bree has been staying with the Stauffer family for some weeks, Simon's brother Andrew doubts what Bree is telling his parents and confronts her with his suspicions.

What will Andrew do when he finds out Bree's secrets?

Will Bree's and Mr. and Mrs. Stauffer's plans be thrown into doubt after another unexpected visitor knocks on their door?

Book 5

Amish Widow's Proposal

Amish woman, Evelyn King, had spent years being disappointed in her husband and her marriage. When Evelyn's husband died, leaving her pregnant and with a three-year-old daughter, she is faced with many problems including a house in ill-repair. When the quiet and kind Hezekiah Hostetler suddenly proposes, Evelyn knows this will solve all her problems as Hezekiah is nothing like her late husband. While pondering on his proposal, a handsome new man visits the community and offers to fix her house.

Can Evelyn put the bitter memories of her past marriage behind her? Or will her fear of abandonment cause her to jump into another unsuitable marriage?

Book 6

The Pregnant Amish Nanny

When Amish woman Courtney Willis is left widowed and expecting a baby, she moves to a larger community in hopes of finding a job and a new life. Courtney is delighted to receive a job as a nanny to an Amish widower who has three unruly children.

Aaron's wife died a year ago and he soon learned it was impossible to hold down his farming responsibilities and look after three children and a household. He's overjoyed when his aunt writes to him letting him know that a suitable Amish woman is on her way. The nanny Aaron pictured was not the one who arrived. He was disturbed to see that Courtney was expecting a child.

Will Courtney be able to persuade Aaron that she'll be able to do it all despite the fact that she will soon have another child to look after?

Can Aaron and Courtney find common ground

and resolve their differences before the arrival of Courtney's baby?

Things grow worse for Courtney with the arrival of Willa, Aaron's sister-in-law, who does all she can to discredit Courtney.

When Courtney's feelings for Aaron start to develop, what will she do when she discovers that Willa is hatching a plot to capture Aaron's heart?

Book 7

A Pregnant Widow's Amish Vacation

When advertising executive, Jane Walker, finds herself widowed and expecting her first child, she sinks into a severe depression.

Her boss and co-workers surprise her with a vacation, forcing her from the safety of her office.

She's too embarrassed to tell anyone her late husband was leaving her for another woman when he was killed in the accident.

When Jane arrives at the vacation destination, she's most upset to find that the B&B is run by an

Amish family.

Jane meets the family's son, Zac, a widower with a young child, and takes an immediate dislike to him.

Why does Jane have a grudge against the Amish?

What will Jane discover about Zac that will forever link them together?

Book 8
The Amish Firefighter's Widow

When Amish woman Katie's volunteer firefighter husband dies while in the line of duty, she is heartbroken. Not only have her two young sons lost their father, but the child she is carrying will never know him. Her husband's best friend, Mark, steps in to take care of Katie and her children.

Many months pass and Mark is offered an opportunity away from Lancaster County. Not wanting to leave Katie and the children behind, he makes his feelings known. Katie tells Mark she would never marry again, and if she did, it would never be to another firefighter. Katie urges him to take the job. Months turn into years before Katie realizes that she has made a terrible mistake. When Mark finally returns, will Katie find that she's left things too late?

Book 9
Amish Widow's Secret

Cassandra Yoder was a girl who never wanted to follow the rules. Soon after Cassandra's boyfriend finds out she's pregnant, he leaves her alone on *rumspringa* and returns to their Amish community. Not long after, he is killed in a shooting. Cassandra considers she has no choice but to return home. When her parents find out she's pregnant, the only solution is to send her to Aunt Maud who will help her find a couple to adopt the baby. When Cassandra meets Reuben, a handsome Amish man, at Aunt Maud's house, she begins to change her mind about many things, including her plans for the baby.

What happens to make Cassandra's new plans come crashing about her?

What will Reuben think when he discovers that Cassandra has lied to him about the real reason she's staying at her aunt's?

With time running out, can Cassandra find a way to keep her baby and the Amish man she's grown to love?

Samantha loves to hear from her readers.
Connect with Samantha at:
samanthaprice333@gmail.com
http://twitter.com/AmishRomance
http://www.facebook.com/SamanthaPriceAuthor

75206096R00126

Made in the USA
Middletown, DE
03 June 2018